It would be so easy to lean down and kiss Joni…

But Carter needed answers first. "Do I make you tremble, Joni?"

She drew in a ragged breath, but didn't answer him.

He slid both of his hands up her arms to her shoulders, kneading away the tension there. "Because you sure as hell shake up my world."

This time he didn't stop himself. When she turned her head away, he leaned in and kissed her neck, his lips resting against her skin as he spoke. "You've got me thinking about things… wanting things…I haven't dared think about before."

He moved up, feathering kisses along her jaw, until he was hovering over her mouth. He pulled her closer, crushing her to him. He kissed the side of her mouth, and then her lips, nipping, licking, suckling, lavishing attention on her sensitive mouth. "I want you," he whispered. "And I'm not going to let you pretend anymore that you don't want me."

She let out a gasp. "Yes," she whispered.

"Yes, what?"

"Yes, I want you!"

Dear Reader,

Do you believe in love at first sight? In finding your soul mate? I'll admit I believe in these things. What can I say—I'm a true romantic.

The hero of this book, Carter Sullivan, started out to be an entirely different type of man. But the moment I wrote his first scene I realized that underneath this experienced street cop was a romantic who believed that Fate would send him the woman of his dreams.

My heroine, Joni Montgomery, thinks finding the right man requires a practical approach, like choosing a financial investment or planning a schedule.

When practical and romantic meet, sparks fly. Whose approach is the right one? Open the book and find out.

I hope you enjoy reading this story as much as I enjoyed writing it. I love to hear from readers. Write to me in care of Harlequin Books, 225 Duncan Mill Road, Don Mills, Ontario, M3B 3K9, Canada, or e-mail me at CindiMyers1@aol.com.

Best wishes,

Cindi Myers

Books by Cindi Meyers

HARLEQUIN TEMPTATION
902—IT'S A GUY THING!

HARLEQUIN BLAZE
82—JUST 4 PLAY

Don't miss any of our special offers. Write to us at the following address for information on our newest releases.

Harlequin Reader Service
U.S.: 3010 Walden Ave., P.O. Box 1325, Buffalo, NY 14269
Canadian: P.O. Box 609, Fort Erie, Ont. L2A 5X3

SAY YOU WANT ME
Cindi Myers

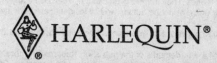

HARLEQUIN®

TORONTO • NEW YORK • LONDON
AMSTERDAM • PARIS • SYDNEY • HAMBURG
STOCKHOLM • ATHENS • TOKYO • MILAN • MADRID
PRAGUE • WARSAW • BUDAPEST • AUCKLAND

For Lynda and Trent.
Thank you, Lynda, for all your help with this one.

ISBN 0-373-69135-1

SAY YOU WANT ME

Printed in U.S.A.

_____Prologue_____

As EMERGENCIES WENT, this one was definitely a Code Blue. Joni Montgomery leaned back against the nurses' station counter at San Antonio's Santa Rosa Hospital and stared at the phone in her hand as if it might morph into an octopus at any moment. After all, things like that happened in nightmares, didn't they? And this couldn't possibly be real.

She put the phone back to her ear and tried to sound calm. "Now, Mama, maybe you misunderstood. G.P. couldn't possibly be coming here this time of year. She's always in Charlotte for the V.A. Air Show."

"I wish I was wrong, but I know what she said. Your grandmother Pettigrew is coming to San Antonio in two weeks and she's staying until she finds you a husband."

Joni ground her teeth and thrust one hand into the pocket of her nurse's smock. She could have sworn she'd stashed some samples of extra-strength headache pills there earlier. All of a sudden, she could feel a mother of a headache coming on. "Why does she have to do this now? In fact, why does she have to do this at all? Doesn't she think I can find my own man?"

"Apparently not. She said she's waited twenty-six years and she's not going to wait any longer for you to find a suitable husband."

Joni squeezed against the counter to allow an EKG cart to pass. "Mama, you *know* the kind of man G.P. thinks is suitable." She closed her eyes, picturing the parade of race-car drivers, fighter pilots and bull riders her grandmother had sent her way. There'd even been one bomb demolition expert. Give a man a dangerous job or a reckless attitude and he was prime husband material as far as G.P. was concerned.

"She thinks you need more excitement in your life."

"Being an emergency department nurse isn't exciting enough?" Joni looked at the row of crash carts ready for use, the curtained exam rooms and the half-dozen doctors and nurses moving busily among them. One Saturday night around this place made a person long for the mundane and ordinary.

"What's wrong with a boring man?" she asked. "You married a boring man." Joni's father was a tax assessor whose idea of excitement was Friday night at the video store.

"Your father may seem boring to you, but he's actually very romantic."

Joni resisted the urge to roll her eyes. Her entire family was addicted to romance, leaving Joni the odd woman out. "Romance is overrated," she said, not for the first time. Other things were much more important in a relationship: dependability, stability, integrity. Things she hadn't found in the right combination yet, but she was sure she would, given time to do things her own way.

"Romance is not overrated to your grandmother. And not to you, if you'd only admit it."

Joni groaned. "I won't do it, Mama. I won't marry some adrenaline junkie just to please G.P."

"You'll have to discuss that with her when she gets here. I only called to warn you."

"Thanks, Mama. For the warning, anyway." She hung up the phone and slumped against the counter. She'd scream, but that tended to upset the patients. So she settled for reaching behind the counter and helping herself to the staff supply of M&M's. Headache pills were fine for some things, but serious crises called for chocolate.

"Joni, we need a hand over here."

Soon, both Joni's hands were occupied giving a breathing treatment to a thirteen-year-old girl who'd had an allergic reaction to peanuts. While she monitored the girl's vitals and waited for the treatment to take effect, Joni considered her options.

She could leave town. But she only had a week's accumulated vacation, and she couldn't afford to travel very far. G.P. would either stay in town until Joni returned or come looking for her.

She could refuse to cooperate. After all, she was a grown woman in the United States of America. The idea of her grandmother choosing a husband for her was ridiculous.

Except that G.P. wrote the book on stubborn. She'd simply smile and keep going her own way, and the next thing Joni knew, she'd be standing at the altar with a motorcycle stunt rider or a professional mountain climber by her side.

She checked the oxygen sensor attached to the girl's index finger. "You're doing really good," she said, patting the child's shoulder. "Keep breathing."

If running away and putting her foot down didn't work, that left one other choice: she had to convince her grandmother that she already had a man in her life. That G.P. didn't have to hunt up a husband for her granddaughter, because marriage was already imminent.

All she had to do was find a guy to hang out with for the week or so G.P. was in town.

She looked around the room for likely candidates. There was that good-looking new resident.... No, residents worked killer hours. Even if he could get an evening free to take her out, he'd likely fall asleep.

The paramedic from Lone Star Ambulance? She made a face. G.P. would love him. He raced motorcycles when he wasn't careening through the streets behind the wheel of an ambulance. No thanks.

Her gaze lit on a policeman at the front desk. He was kind of cute, in those motorcycle boots and tight pants.... No! Definitely not a cop. Cops were the worst adrenaline junkies of all. Her friend Connie had married a cop. And since her husband was always involved in an investigation or doing off-duty work, Connie was practically raising their three sons by herself.

There you had it. The reason she didn't have a man in her life was that all the men she met were too involved in their jobs. She wanted a man who would be there for her and their children—not someone who spent all his time risking his life, even if it was to save mankind.

A plump, curly-haired woman pulled back the curtain and peered into the treatment room. "Mandy, are you okay?"

Mandy, who had been doing just fine until that moment, burst into tears. "Mama!"

The woman rushed forward and gathered the girl in a hug. "I came as soon as the school called."

Joni stepped back to allow mother and daughter a little more privacy. Five years as a nurse hadn't inured her to such scenes. What was more special than the bond between mother and child? It was a bond she intended to experience for herself one day, as soon as she found the right man to stand by her side.

She consulted the chart clipped to the corner of the exam room. "Mandy's going to be fine, Mrs. Wilson. She just needs to stay away from peanuts. The doctor will be in to talk with you in a minute."

She left the room and returned to the nurse's station for a refill of M&M's. That settled it, then. If she couldn't find a man on the job, she'd have to look farther afield.

She glanced at the wall calendar. She had two weeks. Surely she could find a man in two weeks.

1

TWO DAYS. Joni had two days to find a man—any man—to keep Grandmother Pettigrew off her back. She'd exhausted her list of old boyfriends and available male acquaintances in one week and now had resorted to blind dates. If she didn't find a man soon, she was going to end up with a Pamela Pettigrew special and the makings of a full-blown family feud.

She pulled into the restaurant parking lot and checked her hair in the rearview mirror. After enduring dates with a man old enough to be her grandfather, another who ended the evening by asking if he could lick her toes, and a third man who claimed to be the offspring of aliens, she was pulling out all the stops for tonight—mascara *and* eyeliner, vampy red lipstick, and a blue silk minidress that showcased her curves and long legs. She'd curled her hair, painted her nails and spritzed on the expensive French perfume G.P. had given her for Christmas. She had reason to believe this guy might actually be relatively normal, and she wasn't going to let him slip away.

She studied her reflection in the mirror. Not a bad looking chicklet, if she did say so herself. Maybe a little too serious. She tried a smile. There. Didn't she look like a woman who could make a man's dreams come true?

Not that she had any intention of dream fulfillment, but it didn't hurt to give a man aspirations. Besides, this man had to be *the* one. She didn't know how many more blind dates like this she could survive. Her coworker, Marcelle, had sworn her cousin was a nice, ordinary accountant. Thirty years old. Sweet. "Just don't say anything about his hair," Marcelle had cautioned. "It's getting thin and he's sensitive."

Hair or no hair, if he didn't have alien blood or a foot fetish, he was a winner in Joni's book. She slid out of the car and smoothed her skirt over her hips. She didn't have any more time to be picky. Even the sleep-deprived residents at the hospital were beginning to look good.

A blast of air-conditioning and the aroma of garlic and oregano greeted her when she opened the door of the restaurant. She blinked in the dim light. She could just make out a wall lined with wine bottles and a leather upholstered bar to her left. Candles flickered in raffia-covered Chianti bottles on tables draped in red linen.

Her stomach gave a nervous shimmy. She'd chosen this place because it was near her apartment and she liked Italian food, but she hadn't remembered it being so...romantic. What she had in mind was more of a business transaction, not romance.

She hoped her date was already here. What was his name again? Brian?

"May I help you?" The maître d' materialized out of some dark corner and looked down his nose, straight at her cleavage.

She resisted the urge to tug at her dress. "Um, I'm supposed to meet someone here." She tried to see past him, into the dining room.

He moved over to block her view. "Perhaps if you describe this person, I can tell you if they're present or not."

She frowned. Well, of course she couldn't describe him. What had Marcelle said? "He's, uh, he has dark hair and dark eyes. Not too tall. Average."

The maître d' raised one eyebrow. She realized she'd just described half the population of San Antonio. She stared right back. She had even less patience with rude people than she did with daredevils. Not to mention that five years of dealing with medical residents had taught her how to handle men who thought they were superior.

The maître d' turned away. "I'll see if there's anyone here who fits that description."

As soon as he was gone, she moved to the doorway and peered into the dining room. The romantic theme continued here, with grapevines twined around wooden beams and candlelit tables for two. One end of the room had been left empty for a dance floor, a crystal chandelier suspended overhead.

At this early hour, the place was only half full, and

it was easy to spot the only person by himself. A dark-haired, broad-shouldered man in a western-cut sports coat sat at a table on the left side of the room. He looked up from the wine list and she sucked in a deep breath. The men in Marcelle's family must be something else if Marcelle thought this one was ordinary.

He had a strong face, with dark eyes and thick brows, a square jaw and Roman nose. His skin was the weathered bronze of a man who spent a lot of time outdoors. Fine lines radiated from the corners of his eyes and a small scar to the right of his mouth kept him from being too pretty. He had nice lips—the kind that looked as if they knew how to kiss a woman.

She blinked. Where had that come from? This was a blind date. Who said anything about kissing? She squared her shoulders and took a deep breath. She had one goal tonight: to convince this man to accompany her to a family barbecue and pose as her boyfriend.

If it took kissing to do that...well, a girl had to make some sacrifices, didn't she?

CARTER SULLIVAN stared into his glass of wine and listened to the Italian folk songs emanating from the speakers overhead. What was the expression? Wine, women and song. He sighed. Maybe two out of three wasn't bad.... No, it *was* bad. Because he couldn't remember the last time he'd had a date. His job didn't leave a lot of time to meet eligible women.

Or, if he was honest, he could admit he hadn't made the effort lately to get off his ass and find Ms. Right. Busting auto thieves and chasing down muggers was less daunting to him than playing the dating game. If the rejection didn't get you, the emotional roller-coaster ride would. Most of the time it was easier to stay on the sidelines and hope that fate would send someone his way.

Which meant a lot of evenings like this one, where a craving for manicotti like Mama Calabria made had brought him to Trattoria Fabrizio. He poured another glass of Chianti and raised it in a silent toast. *To Ms. Right. Wherever you are.*

He blinked at the image of a woman that appeared in the glass in his hand. The kind of woman fantasies are made of. He shook his head, trying to clear it, and wondered if it was time to switch to water.

When he looked again, he saw that the image was a reflection of a real woman, who was walking toward him. She looked even better in real life than she had in his glass, with long strawberry-blond hair, legs a Las Vegas showgirl would envy and a figure that made every man in the room put down his fork to watch her walk by.

Carter rose when she stopped at his table. "Hello. I'm sorry I kept you waiting," she said. She pulled out the chair across from him and sat. "I didn't think I was running this late."

"That's quite all right." He sat also, unable to stop staring at her. If the fates really had sent this woman to him, they couldn't have done a better job. Up close, she had skin like porcelain, delicate features, and large blue eyes framed by thick lashes. Bedroom eyes. He let his vision move lower, to the generous breasts swelling at the neckline of her little blue dress, and the belt cinching her trim waist. Yes, this was his fantasy woman all right.

Any minute now, he'd wake up and reality would come crashing down around him, but while the fantasy lasted, he intended to enjoy himself. "Would you like some wine?" he asked.

"Yes, that would be nice."

He signaled the waiter for a glass and poured for her, then topped up his own glass. "I'm sorry, I didn't catch your name," he said.

She smiled. "Didn't Marcelle tell you? It's Joni. Joni Montgomery."

He nodded. "Pleased to meet you, Joni. I'm Carter. Carter Sullivan."

She froze with the wineglass halfway to her lips. "I thought your name was Brian."

Ahh. So she was someone else's fantasy after all. Well, whoever this Brian character was, he was going to have to wait his turn. "No, it's Carter."

"I must have misunderstood." She sipped the wine. "To tell you the truth, I've had a lot my mind lately." She glanced at him. "I don't know how much Marcelle told you about my situation."

"Marcelle didn't tell me anything." Which was, of course, absolutely true.

The waiter arrived with two gold-tasseled menus. Carter pretended to read his while studying her. No rings on her fingers. Tasteful but expensive gold earrings. Neatly trimmed nails and a plain gold watch. Classy, not flashy. Exactly the kind of woman he favored.

The way she was staring, he wasn't sure he'd made such a great impression on her. "Is something wrong?" he asked.

She flushed, a rosy glow like candlelight against ivory. "It's just...your hair. It's not thin at all!"

He put one hand to his head. When he was younger, he'd complained because his hair was thick and hard to style, but now he was at the age where he was grateful it was all there. He grinned at her. "No, it's not. Guess I'm lucky that way." He sat up a little straighter. So she liked his hair. That was a start.

The waiter arrived to take their order. She had the chicken piccata while he went with the manicotti. "You said something about your situation?" he prompted when they were alone again.

"Oh yes." She smoothed her napkin in her lap. "Well, I don't usually go on blind dates. I mean, not that it isn't a perfectly nice way to meet people but...well, to tell you the truth, I'm so busy I really haven't had much time to date."

"Believe me, I understand." He sipped his wine. "What do you do?"

"Marcelle didn't tell you that either?" She laughed. "I'm going to have to talk to that girl. I'm a nurse. She and I work together in the emergency department at Santa Rosa Hospital." She smiled at him. "And I understand you're an accountant."

He was tempted to go along with the story, but he'd always been a lousy liar. "Actually, I'm a cop," he said.

Her smile melted away and something like anger flashed in her eyes. "You're joking, aren't you?"

He shook his head. "'Fraid not." He took out his wallet and flashed his I.D. and flat badge. "San Antonio's finest, at your service."

She sat back, silent for a long moment, staring into the wine. Carter wondered if now was the time to come clean with the whole story—that he didn't know Marcelle, or the missing Brian, and that he wasn't her blind date for the evening, though he'd gladly volunteer for the job.

She began to chuckle. "What's so funny?" he asked.

"I just realized, this must be Marcelle's idea of a joke. She knows how I feel about cops."

He stiffened. "And how is that?"

She blushed again, a deeper red. "Oh, I didn't mean anything by that. I'm sure you're a very nice person. I just don't want to date a cop. I mean...not usually."

He was saved from having to respond by the arrival of their dinner. As he silently ate his manicotti, he was acutely aware of the beautiful woman seated across from him. His fantasy woman who didn't want to date a cop. It figured.

She pushed her chicken piccata around on her plate, not eating. "Is something wrong with the food?" he asked.

"No. No, it's delicious." She pushed her plate away and looked at him. "I'm sorry. I've really gotten off on the wrong foot, haven't I? Can we start again?" She held out her hand. "Hi, I'm Joni Montgomery."

He smiled and took her hand. "Pleased to meet you, Joni. I'm Carter Sullivan."

"My pleasure, Carter." They sat there like that for a long moment, smiling and holding hands. Carter felt a surge of something like hope. Maybe this night had some magic in it after all....

"Excuse me, did you say your name was Joni Montgomery?" A short, balding man in a three-piece suit approached their table.

Joni turned to him. "Yes?"

"I'm Brian Anderson. Marcelle's cousin."

JONI STARED at the man. Short...balding...three-piece suit...he even had Marcelle's squint. She looked again at the man across from her. Tall...gorgeous hair...a sports coat he filled out to perfection. What had she been thinking? This wasn't a man who needed a cousin to fix him up with a date. Women probably followed him around like puppies.

So what was he doing sitting across from her now?

"I...I can explain," he said.

"Oh, and you will," she muttered. She turned to Brian. "I'm terribly sorry, there must have been some mix-up." She glanced at Carter, then back at Marcelle's cousin. Should she stay or go? After all, Brian was her *real* date. But she and Carter had been having such a nice time. Brian was probably nice, too, but what if he wasn't? She was running out of time to find a man who could convince G.P. to leave well enough alone. She looked at Carter again. Did she stick with a known danger—a very handsome danger at that—or try the unknown danger, who might very well turn out to be another toe-licking alien?

Carter chose that moment to wink, a slow, seductive lowering of one eyelid that sent a hot shiver through her. She swallowed and turned back to Brian, giving him her best smile. "Um, I must have gotten my days mixed up. Maybe we could try again some other night?" Marcelle wouldn't be happy about this, but Joni would think of something to tell her.

"Oh, well..." Brian glanced at Carter, who sat with arms folded across his chest, silent challenge in his eyes. "Uh, yeah. Maybe some other time." Brian backed away from the table. "Uh, guess I'll go now."

When he was gone, Carter refilled her wineglass. "What now?" he asked.

She leaned forward, elbows on the table. "Now, you explain. Why didn't you speak up when you realized what was happening?"

He smiled. A devastating grin that warmed her like

a shot of good brandy. "Imagine you're a man sitting in a restaurant, down in the mouth because once again you're eating alone. Suddenly, a beautiful woman sits down at your table and announces she's your date." He shook his head. "I haven't learned many lessons in my life, but I know that when the fates hand you a gift like that, you shut up and take it."

His words sent another tremor through her middle. No one had ever referred to her as a gift before. She ran her fingers up and down the stem of her wineglass. "I'd think a cop would be too hard-nosed to believe in something as ephemeral as fate."

"Then you'd be wrong. My persistence in believing nothing happens by chance has kept me safe and sane out there on the streets."

The streets where he got his thrills chasing down the bad guys. Of course, somebody had to do that job, but that didn't mean *she* had to get involved with them. "I still think you should have said something when I first showed up."

"You're here now. Your accountant is gone. We might as well enjoy ourselves." As if on cue, a new song began. Carter offered his hand. "Would you like to dance?"

She stared at his outstretched fingers. "I...I don't know how." What a shameful thing for a grown woman to admit. G.P. had sent her to dance class when she was in junior high school, but Joni had played hooky every week, preferring to visit the zoo instead.

Carter stood and pulled her up beside him. "That's all right. I'll show you."

Reluctantly, she allowed him to lead her onto the dance floor. G.P. would probably say her lack of dancing ability was one reason she was still single, but who had time for something as old-fashioned as dance lessons?

Apparently Carter Sullivan had taken the time. He moved with the assurance of someone at home on the dance floor. One hand rested at the small of her back, strong and reassuring, while the other helped to guide her in the steps. He leaned closer and whispered in her ear. "Relax. Feel the music."

But all she could feel was *him*. His body pressed against hers, warm and strong, muscular without being overbearing. She could easily imagine this powerful man chasing down robbers, rescuing children, and performing all sorts of other heroic acts.

She'd obviously had too much wine if she was letting herself get caught up in such a romantic fantasy. After all, she knew well enough that for every hero spotlighted on the nightly news, there were loved ones standing in the shadows. And when the heroics were all over, the wife and kids were the ones who got hurt.

"Hey, it's not that bad, is it?" He put his finger under her chin and tilted her head up. "You look like you lost your best friend."

She raised her eyes to meet his, and too late realized her mistake. He had beautiful eyes—not black, but dark blue, almost violet. They looked at her with an intensity that made her feel, not physically undressed, but emotionally naked.

She looked away again, at her feet, and stumbled against him. "It's all right," he soothed, and pulled her closer.

She fought the urge to rest her head on his shoulder, to savor the feeling of his arms around her. Despite her misgivings about his profession, she had to admit that Carter Sullivan was one-hundred-percent attractive male. The kind of man any woman would admire.

"G.P. would love you," she murmured.

He blinked. "Who is G.P.?"

She sighed. Now was as good a time as any for the story to come out. "G.P. is my grandmother Pettigrew. She never seemed like an ordinary grandmother to me when I was growing up, so I called her G.P."

The music stopped and he led her back to the table. The dinner dishes had been cleared, replaced by a carafe of coffee and two demitasse cups. "I take it your grandmother likes cops?"

"Cops. Firemen. Soldiers. Pilots. Race-car drivers. If a job is dangerous or daring, she's in love."

"But she didn't pass this love to her granddaughter." His expression was serious, but his eyes laughed at her.

She added sugar to her cup. "Let's just say I prefer someone who's more...stable."

He nodded. "That's me, all right. Mr. Unstable. It's a wonder they let me on the force."

She made a face. "I get your point and I'm not going to argue with you. In fact, I hope you'll agree to help me with something."

His gaze on her had the intensity of a physical touch. "I'm listening."

She leaned toward him, looking into his eyes. "Carter, I need a man. I need you."

CARTER SWALLOWED HARD, sure he was back in dream world. Wasn't this the same woman who'd said she didn't like cops? Then again, she *had* chosen to stay with him instead of the accountant. And she hadn't exactly protested when they'd cuddled up on the dance floor. He grinned. "So my devastating charm has won you over."

She picked up a coffee spoon and studied her reflection in it. "Do you remember when I told you I had a lot on my mind?"

"Yes, and you were going to tell me about it, but you never got around to it."

She glanced around them. "Let's go somewhere a little more private and I'll explain everything."

He wasn't too surprised when she tried to pay the check, but he pushed her credit card back into her hand. "Call me old-fashioned, but I'll pay."

She frowned. "That's ridiculous. This wasn't even your idea."

When the waiter returned, Carter signed the credit card slip and tore off his copy. "Let's just say my fragile male ego will be crushed if I let a beautiful woman, whose company I've enjoyed by the way, pick up the check."

He wasn't surprised to find her blushing again. Maybe he hadn't lost his touch after all.

He walked her to her car. "Where do you want to go?" he asked.

"Here is fine." She leaned against the driver's-side door, facing him. "It's just that this story is kind of embarrassing and I didn't want anyone to overhear."

"The suspense is killing me." He shoved his hands into his pockets, though what he really wanted to do was hold her again.

She fiddled with a row of beads on her key chain. "In two days, my grandmother Pettigrew is coming to San Antonio for the sole purpose of finding a husband for me."

He chuckled. "You're not serious."

"Serious as a heart attack. G.P. has decided it's time I was married and once she makes a decision, there's no stopping her."

"Where do I come in?" He stood up straighter. "Not as the potential groom?"

"No!" She dropped the keys and stooped to retrieve them, but he got them first.

He returned the keys to her. "No bridegroom."

She nodded. "No, but I want you to pretend to be my boyfriend, just for a few days. You could come to the barbecue we're having in her honor." She met his gaze again. "Once she meets you, she'll realize her services aren't needed."

So she wanted him, but only long enough to fool her grandmother. Should he be insulted, or pleased? A man with more pride would probably tell her to find some other guy for her charade.

But a man with more pride would end up alone. Why not take the chance to spend more time with the woman fate had sent his way?

"What's in it for me?" he asked.

"The chance to do a good deed? Free barbecue?"

He shook his head.

She frowned. "What do you want?"

"I want you to give me a chance to prove that a cop can be relationship material. That whatever opinion you've formed about me is wrong."

"You won't change my mind."

"Oh, but I'll enjoy the challenge." He put his hands on her shoulders. "After this is over, go out with me again. Not just to pull one over on your grandmother, but on a real date. For yourself."

She looked away, her lips in a tight line. He could almost see her weighing the pros and cons of his proposal. But where was she going to find another guy to agree to her crazy plan on such short notice? She must have reached the same conclusion. "All right. I guess I can do that."

"Good. Then what say we start right this minute?"

She looked wary. "How?"

"With a good-night kiss."

Her eyes widened in surprise as he brought his lips to hers. He slipped his arms around her, pressing her tightly against his chest, stroking her back in a soothing motion as his mouth teased away her resistance.

He kissed the corners of her mouth and traced his tongue along the seam of her lips, then bent to kiss the tender flesh of her throat, her skin like satin against his tongue. He returned to her mouth, sucking gently at her lips, every sensitive nerve of his own mouth alive to her.

Triumph filled him as she melted against him, and her lips parted. She tasted of the wine they'd shared and smelled of exotic flowers. And she felt…God, she felt like heaven. He moved his hand to her waist, bringing her closer against his erection. He wanted her to know how she affected him. Instead of drawing away, she pressed into him, her hands on his back, fingers digging in.

Somewhere nearby, a car door slammed, making him aware that they were in a public place. Reluctantly, he drew away, and tried to catch his breath.

She leaned back against the car, eyes glazed, lips swollen and slightly parted, hair mussed. She truly looked like a woman in need of a man now, and given the slightest encouragement, he'd have been happy to oblige. He clenched his fists, hoping she wouldn't see his hands shaking.

He saw the moment reason returned to her, watched her face pale and her eyes widen. She straightened and smoothed her hands over her hair, down her dress. "I...I'd better go." She turned and fumbled with her keys, missing the door lock completely.

He stepped forward and took them from her hand, opened the door for her, then leaned in and fit the key in the ignition. "Maybe you'd better sit here a minute before you drive home," he said.

She slid into the driver's seat and shook her head. "No. I'm fine."

He wished she'd look at him. He put his hand on her shoulder. "Listen, I didn't mean for things to get so carried away just now."

She nodded, still avoiding his eyes.

"But I think maybe it means something. Maybe we're not such a bad match after all."

"I think you shouldn't read more into this than there is, Mr. Sullivan." She turned the key in the ignition, starting the engine. "Unlike you, I don't believe in fate."

He had to leap back as she slammed the door. Then she sped out of the parking lot, in violation of half a dozen traffic laws. He stared after her, then started to chuckle. Oh, she was a pistol all right. He was going to enjoy proving to her how wrong she was about fate. And about them.

2

JONI WOKE the next morning from a restless sleep, thinking of Carter. How was it possible for a man she scarcely knew to disturb her so? Surely she'd never met anyone who infuriated her more. Take that whole business of him paying for dinner. Fragile male ego—hah! He was about as fragile as a concrete wall.

And that kiss—that incredible, mind-blowing kiss. He'd just assumed she'd *wanted* him to kiss her. Yeah, so she'd enjoyed the kiss. It probably ranked among the top five kisses she'd received in her lifetime. Maybe even number one. That kiss had lit up every nerve in her body like Fourth of July fireworks.

But that was beside the point. Any woman would be physically attracted to a man like Carter. She still knew better than to get involved with him. After all, he was a cop. A man addicted to the power trip of being an authority figure and hooked on the danger rush that went along with the badge. A man who would leave a wife and children at home while he went out the door every day to put his life on the line. Not the kind of man she wanted as a husband and father to her children.

He'd spouted all that nonsense about fate. She didn't believe in fate. A person had to be responsible for her own life. Make her own choices. Something she'd been trying to tell G.P. since she was ten years old and her grandmother had made her take those stupid dance lessons.

She sighed. Okay, maybe they weren't so stupid. Maybe it would be nice to learn to dance. But because she wanted to, not because G.P. or anybody else thought it was a good idea.

You sound like a two-year-old. Her conscience jabbed her, and she frowned at her face in the bathroom mirror. It was too early in the morning to grapple with her conscience. A grown woman ought to be able to declare her independence without sounding like a toddler. The point was, she *didn't, didn't, didn't* want to get involved with a man like Carter Sullivan.

Which took her back to the problem of what to do about G.P. and her plans to see her granddaughter happily married. She wrestled with this dilemma while she munched down a bowl of cereal and packed her lunch. By the time she arrived at work, she knew she had only one real choice.

She found the number for the San Antonio Police Department in the phone book and asked to speak to Officer Carter Sullivan. The operator transferred her to the patrol sergeant. "Officer Sullivan isn't in right now," the sergeant told her. "Can I help you with something?"

"No, I...can I leave a message for him?"

"I can put you through to his voice mail. Are you one of his kids?"

"Uh, no."

"Uh, okay. Well, here's his voice mail."

Kids? All the breath rushed out of her. Carter had kids? What else had he failed to mention last night? An ex-wife...or several? Not that they'd gone into much depth about their backgrounds, but you would think a man would remember something as important as children....

"You've reached the voice mailbox of Officer Carter Sullivan. Leave a message..."

"Uh, Carter, this is Joni Montgomery," she stammered. "Call me." Then she recited her phone number.

She returned to the nurses' station and tried to concentrate on work, but thoughts of Carter kept intruding. Thoughts of that incredible kiss. Memories of him holding her. *Would you get out of my head?* she wanted to shout.

"Joni, there's someone here to see you," a nurse told her before headed down the hall.

She looked up from her charts at a broad-shouldered man in the crisp blue uniform of a San Antonio police officer. Her heart did a back flip and she felt the blood rush to her face. How was she supposed to deal with Carter calmly when her body reacted so fiercely to him?

"I get a kick out of the way you blush so easily." He

grinned and moved closer to the nurses' station. "I didn't think women did that anymore."

"Blushing is merely an involuntary physical reaction." She busied herself straightening a stack of patient charts that didn't need straightening. "Like hiccups, or sweaty palms."

"Hmm. More attractive, though. Especially on you."

She could feel his gaze like a hot caress on her skin. When she raised her head, she found him regarding her with a half smile on his lips that would have made a nun have second thoughts about her vocation. "What are you doing here?" she asked.

"You forgot to tell me how to get in touch with you. Then I remembered you said you worked at Santa Rosa. I took a chance you'd be here today."

"I just called and left you a message at the station."

His smile broadened. "Then you didn't chicken out."

She'd wanted to, but she hadn't been able to think of any other way to appease G.P. Or any other man who would be sure to have her grandmother packing her bags and heading out of Texas in short order. "We made an agreement. I intend to keep my part of it." After all, how hard could it be to endure one date with him?

"I stopped by to find out what the plan is for tomorrow night, and so we could get our stories straight before the big event."

"Speaking of getting stories straight..." She moved

out from behind the nurses' station. "Let's go back to the break room for a minute and talk about a few things."

The closet-size room at the end of the hall had just enough space for a table and two chairs, a small refrigerator and a cart that held a microwave, a coffeemaker, and assorted boxes of crackers, cans of coffee and jars of tea bags. A half-empty box of donuts sat on the table.

Joni shut the door behind them and turned to face him. "Why didn't you mention last night that you have children?"

His smile vanished. "What the hell?" He stared at her, true astonishment on his face. "I don't have any children. Where did you get an idea like that?"

She clutched the back of a folding chair. "When I called the station, the man who answered asked if I was one of your kids."

Laughter exploded from him. She tightened her grip on the chair. "What's so funny about that?"

Carter shook his head. "He wasn't talking about my children."

"Then who was he talking about?"

He shoved his hands in his pockets. "The area I patrol attracts a lot of street kids. Runaways. I try to get to know them—let them know if they ever need anything, they can call me."

"Street kids." Her heart gave a little twist. "That...that's really nice of you."

"Yeah, that's me. A regular saint." He cocked one

eyebrow. "Sorry to disappoint you. I know you were expecting worse things from me."

Touché. She looked at the floor. "You're right. I'm sorry."

"So what's the deal here?" He leaned toward her, his hands on the table between them. "Did you date a cop once and he did you wrong? Did you have a run-in with a bad cop once upon a time? Did your parents threaten to turn you over to the police when you were little and you were bad? Or do you just not like the cut of the uniform?" He looked down at his blue shirt and pants. "I hear women really go for the brown sheriff's department getup. Maybe I should try that."

She bit back a smile. Did they teach cops how to ask serious questions in such a nonthreatening manner? No, she'd bet this particular approach was a Carter Sullivan original. "The uniform is great," she said. And he looked great in it. Every female in the emergency department, including one woman lying on a stretcher, had checked him out when he walked in.

She crossed her arms under her breasts. "I don't like adrenaline junkies."

He straightened and drew his eyebrows together. "Try that one again."

"You know. Men who get off on danger. Cops. Firefighters. Test pilots. Race-car drivers."

"So the danger thing doesn't turn you on?"

Why did he put the question that way? This had nothing to do with sex. "Men into those things are selfish."

He rubbed his chin, considering. "How do you figure that? Haven't you heard the term 'public servant'?"

She shifted her weight to one hip. "I'm not saying you don't provide a public service, or that what you do isn't important. But nobody stays in that kind of work long if they don't get a rush from courting danger. Only, when they get hurt—and odds are they will—their families are the ones who pay the price."

He nodded. "So you figure you'll just avoid that hurt altogether and stick with nice, safe guys. Like accountants."

"That's it." Her shoulders relaxed. Maybe he did understand.

"What if I told you I pulled an accountant out of a wrecked car just two days ago? Head-on collision with a dump truck."

"I'd say it sounded like a story you made up to prove a point."

Laughter lit his eyes. "Okay, so it was a shoe salesman. Same difference."

"The odds are still in the accountant's—or the shoe salesman's—favor."

He moved around the table to stand in front of her, uncomfortably close. "So love to you is a matter of playing the odds?"

She raised her chin, staring past his shoulder, and tried not to breathe too deeply of his leather-and-soap scent. "Who says I can't love a safe man as much as a danger junkie?"

"That's only if we really get to choose who we love."

She jerked her gaze to his. Why did he look so sure of himself? So certain *he* was right. "Of course we do. That's what the whole dating thing is about. Choosing."

He shook his head. "Uh-uh. Love's not like that at all."

"Who made you an expert?"

He stepped closer, backing her up against the door. She couldn't move away without pressing against him, could scarcely draw a breath without the tips of her breasts brushing his chest. But more than his physical proximity, his gaze held her, silencing her protests, stealing thought. "So when you kissed me last night, it was because you chose to do so?"

She swallowed. "Of course."

He leaned over and pressed his lips to her throat, barely catching her flesh between his teeth. Heat knifed through her, melting a path from his mouth to between her legs. "And when you practically came in my arms, it's because you chose to do so." His voice rumbled through her, making her heart pound.

"I did not...do that."

He raised his head to meet her eyes once more. "You were turned on though. I'll bet you were soaking wet."

If he only knew... She closed her eyes against his penetrating gaze and shivered as his mouth moved down her throat to her collarbone, trailing heat along the V neck of her uniform top. "Physical reaction...is different...from love," she gasped.

"Maybe. Let's call it lust then." He cupped her right breast in his palm. "Tell me you're not lusting after me right now."

"Of...of course not."

He ran his thumb across her erect nipple, sending shock waves rippling through her. "Liar."

She tried to pull back, but only managed to flatten herself against the door. "What if I am? It doesn't mean anything."

"Then it won't hurt to act on those feelings." He put his hands on either side of her, flat against the door. "If I locked this door and we went after it right now, it wouldn't make any difference in how you looked at me tomorrow?"

She glared at him. "You do that and I won't be looking at you at all tomorrow."

He stepped back, startling her with the suddenness of the movement. She sagged against the door, shaken and panting. She didn't know whether to be angry at him for putting her in this position, or for leaving her like this, hungry for more.

"I will never force you to do anything," he said, retreating to the table. "But don't lie about what you're feeling either. If you want me, don't be afraid to say so."

Of all the conceited, arrogant— She glared at him. "In your dreams."

He grinned. "Oh, you're already there, sugar." He

fished a donut from the box on the table and took a bite. "So what time is Grandma's get-together tomorrow?"

His question cut off the biting remark forming in her head. She blinked. Was he changing the subject to unsettle her further, or to give her time to cool off?

She thought his fingers trembled as he raised the donut to his lips again and she held back a smile. Maybe he was giving them both time to calm down. "It starts at five o'clock, though my dad will probably be up at five that morning to start the brisket cooking."

"What time do you want me to pick you up?"

She rubbed her arms. She hadn't planned on letting him know where she lived. That made this all too personal. "I thought you could meet me at my parents'."

He shook his head. "That won't work. Not if we're supposed to be crazy in love. We should show up together."

She frowned. "I don't see what difference it makes."

"You want to convince your grandmother, don't you?" He wiped his hands with a paper napkin. "I'll pick you up and we'll come in, the inseparable lovebirds. Your grandmother will go home satisfied you've found the perfect man at last."

"Don't get too far into the role, okay?" She scribbled her address onto another napkin and handed it to him.

He read it and stuffed it into his pocket. "What should I say when people ask how we met?"

"That's easy. Tell them we met at the hospital. Cops come in here all the time."

"And we've been dating how long?"

"Six weeks."

"I'm a fast worker, huh?"

"G.P. knew my grandfather six weeks when they got married."

"How long were they married?"

"Forty-one years."

He laughed. "And you don't believe in fate!"

"G.P. and Grandpa were lucky. That doesn't happen very often." She didn't want to talk about her grandparents' marriage with him. She opened the door. "I have to get back to work."

He stopped and kissed her cheek on his way out. "I'll see you tomorrow evening. I'm looking forward to it."

She stared after him, still feeling the warmth where his lips had been. One moment she was furious with him, and the next he did something that made her positively melt. He'd crashed into her quiet, ordered life like a meteorite. She figured the sooner they ended their deal and parted company, the better off she'd be.

His earlier words to her echoed in the back of her mind (or was that her conscience again?): Liar.

CARTER ARRIVED at Joni's apartment promptly at 4:45, having circled the block half a dozen times to avoid showing up too early. He ate half a pack of breath mints while he was waiting and cranked the air conditioner full blast, praying his antiperspirant didn't fail. Though he hoped he didn't show it, his stomach was in knots at the thought of meeting Joni's family, especially the infamous G.P.

He didn't have much experience with families, though as a cop he'd seen plenty of family feuds gone wrong. If the rest of the family was anything like prickly Joni, he'd have one hell of a time keeping his cool tonight. But he intended to give it his best shot. Joni might be difficult at times, but he couldn't shake the feeling that the two of them could make some magic together. Call it destiny, fate, or mere coincidence, but Joni had come into his life from out of nowhere, and he wasn't about to let her leave too soon.

She greeted him at the door, dressed in an orange tank top and white shorts. He had a tough time not staring, and had to continually pull his gaze away from her long, tanned legs and soft curves. "You look great," he said.

She smiled and surveyed his jeans, boots and knit polo. "You clean up pretty good yourself."

"I brought you something." He handed her a pink rabbit's foot key chain.

"What's this for?" She inspected the rabbit's foot.

"For luck. You said you don't believe in it, but the rabbit's foot works whether you believe or not."

She laughed. "All right. I'll humor you." She clipped the key chain to her purse. "Are you ready?"

He took a deep breath. "I'm ready. By the end of the evening, your grandmother will love me." *And maybe her granddaughter's feelings will be a little more affectionate as well.*

The drive to her parents' home in Alamo Heights took only a few minutes. The house was already surrounded by cars, and a trio of little girls chased each other across the front lawn. "You have a big family," he said.

"Not that big. I have three brothers, Matt, Greg and David. Then there are their wives and children—the girls on the lawn belong to Greg and Matt. David has a baby boy. Aunt Lisa and Uncle Richard will probably be here, and my cousins Marcus and Larry. Uncle Leo and Aunt Lucy, and their sons, Bruce and Peter. Bruce's wife Penny and their two boys, Zach and Thomas..."

"Like I said. A big family. Must be nice." He found a parking space down the street and guided the car in. "Three brothers, huh? So you're the only girl. And the youngest, I'll bet."

"David is younger, but, yeah, I'm the only girl."

He grinned. "No wonder you don't like being bossed around."

She stuck her tongue out at him. He was still chuckling when they walked through the front door. The roomful of people fell silent. He looked at her and saw the telltale flush creeping up her neck. "You didn't tell them you were bringing me, did you?"

She gave him a look of apology. "I, uh, I forgot."

A woman in her fifties with Joni's eyes moved toward them. "Well, don't just stand there. Come in!" She took Carter's arm and led him farther into the room.

"Mama, I'd like you to meet Carter Sullivan. Carter, this is my mother, Adele Montgomery."

"It's a pleasure to meet you," Carter said. "I'd have known you for Joni's mother anywhere."

"And I'm Joni's grandmother." A thin, angular woman with a thick crown of snow-white hair inserted herself between them and offered her hand. "Pamela Pettigrew, but everyone here calls me G.P."

"Pleased to meet you, G.P." Carter shook hands with the old woman, who had a surprisingly strong grip.

She kept hold of his hand and looked him over, starting at the polished toes of his boots and ending at the top of his head. He tried not to squirm, though he had the feeling he was being sized up like a side of beef. G.P. turned to Joni, who stood with her fists clenched at her sides. "Why have you been keeping this man a secret?"

"Well, I, uh..." She looked at him, telegraphing panic.

He put his arm around her. "I think Joni wanted to be sure of my feelings before she sprung me on the whole family."

G.P.'s eyes narrowed. "And what are your feelings?"

He leaned closer and spoke in a confiding tone. "Just between you and me—I love her."

He'd meant the words as a dramatic gesture, but a sudden tightness in his chest when he glanced at Joni told him they might be true. This beautiful, aggravating woman had gotten under his skin in a hurry.

JONI STARED AT HIM, openmouthed. Why had he thought it necessary to say something like that? Especially with her whole family watching and grinning like kids at the circus.

She slid her gaze over to G.P. Her grandmother was still holding Carter's hand, studying him with considerable interest. "Come sit over here and tell me something about yourself," she said, leading him to the sofa.

Aunts Lisa and Lucy moved over to make room, so that Carter ended up sandwiched between G.P. and the grinning aunts. "Tell me how you and Joni met," G.P. said.

Carter leaned back against the sofa cushions, long legs stretched in front of him. Joni stood behind her mother's chair, while the rest of the family arranged themselves around the room. Carter glanced at Joni, then delivered his lines: "I was sitting at a restaurant all alone, depressed because I didn't have someone special in my life, and all of a sudden, this beautiful woman walks right over and sits down at my table."

Joni gasped, drawing curious looks from those near her. She dabbed at her eyes with her fingers, pretending to be all choked up. In reality, she was furious. What did he think he was doing, telling her family the truth?

"She'd mistaken me for the man she was supposed to meet at the restaurant," Carter continued. "One look and I knew fate had sent me the woman I'd been waiting for. We talked all evening, and I guess you could say we really hit it off."

"What a romantic story." Aunt Lucy sighed.

"When was this meeting?" G.P. asked. "How long have you known each other?"

Joni held her breath. If he dared tell the truth this time...

Carter smiled fondly at her. "Six weeks."

A collective sigh issued from her entire sappily romantic family. G.P. beamed. "That's how long my late husband George and I knew each other when we got married." She touched Carter's hand. "We had a wonderful forty-one years together."

"So Joni tells me."

"I wish you could have known him. He was a wonderful man, so full of life. When I met him, he was a barnstorming pilot, flying around to small towns and performing stunts. Our first date, he took me up in his plane and performed two barrel rolls and a backward loop. I knew right then, he was the man for me."

"He sounds like quite a daredevil." Carter had the audacity to wink at Joni.

"Oh, he was. He flew in Korea and worked as a crop duster in the Rio Grande Valley, then flew reconnaissance for Customs. On weekends, we'd go to air shows and he'd fly stunts for fun." She patted his hand. "But you didn't come here to listen to an old woman talk. I want to know about you. What kind of work do you do?"

"I'm a patrol officer with the San Antonio Police Department."

G.P.'s laugh was closer to a cackle. She looked at Joni. "Is that so? What did I tell you?"

Joni crossed her arms over her chest. "I'm not happy about his job."

"I predict you'll get over that soon enough." She turned back to Carter. "Now tell me about your family. Where do they live?"

"I don't really have a family. I grew up in several different foster homes. I stayed the longest with the Calabrias, five years when I was in junior high and high school. I still see them from time to time."

Joni felt like she'd swallowed hummingbirds. She thought of the runaways and homeless kids Carter said he tried to help. Did he see himself and his own childhood when he looked at them?

"You can consider us your family now," G.P. announced. "I always said Joni needed a strong man who could show her how to really live." She leaned toward Carter and lowered her voice, though not so low Joni couldn't hear. "She has a tendency to guard her feelings too well," she said. "Maybe you can teach her to take a few more risks."

He nodded solemnly. "Maybe I can."

Joni turned away. Really, this was getting ridiculous. Carter was acting like this was all real, instead of a ploy to fool her grandmother.

A few minutes later, Carter caught up with her in the kitchen, where she was helping her cousin Bruce slice onions and pickles. "Everything's going pretty good, huh?" he said softly, helping himself to a pickle slice. Bruce was arguing baseball scores with their cousin Marcus.

"Why did you tell them how we really met?"

"Because I'm a lousy liar. Besides, the truth is a better story. I think it really won them over."

She made a face. "Oh, G.P. loves you."

"I like her, too. I like all your family."

She concentrated on making perfect, even slices. "I didn't know that...about your family. I guess that's kind of rough, huh?"

Carter shrugged. "That's the hand I was dealt."

She laid aside the knife and dried her hands on a dish towel. "Don't you have any disgusting habits or annoying traits I can dislike without feeling guilty?"

He laughed. "I can swear in three languages, though that can sometimes be an asset. I can cuss out people in Italian and they don't know if I'm dissing them or ordering spaghetti."

She fought hard to hold back a smile. He slipped his arm around her waist and pulled her close, so he could whisper in her ear. "I wouldn't call it annoying, but I do have the very *frustrating* habit of getting turned on whenever I'm around you."

She wanted to scold him and remind him theirs was supposed to be a business agreement, but when she opened her mouth, all that came out was giggles. Honestly! What was happening to her?

Her father stuck his head in the back door. "Hey, can you two lovebirds break it up long enough for Carter to come out here and play a game of horseshoes? I've already beaten everybody else."

"You haven't beaten the horseshoe champ of the SAPD West Substation." Carter released her and followed her dad into the backyard.

Joni leaned back against the counter and sighed. Carter didn't act like any cop she'd ever known—like any *man* she'd ever known. He was strong, but soft at the same time. He wasn't afraid of revealing himself. After all, what kind of man stood up in front of a bunch of people he'd just met and declared his love for a woman?

Even if it was only an act?

3

EVEN THOUGH Carter and Joni were seated directly across the picnic table from one another, Joni refused to look at him. That's how he knew he was getting to her. Every time he glanced up, her eyes darted away and she pretended a deep interest in the potato salad. You didn't work that hard at avoiding someone's gaze unless you secretly craved it. He grinned and leaned toward her. "The potato salad is excellent, isn't it?"

"Huh?" Her head jerked up and her eyes met his for a split second before focusing somewhere over his left shoulder. He didn't think he'd ever get enough of looking into those eyes, trying to discover all the things they'd teach him about her.

"The potato salad? You were so engrossed in it, I thought maybe it was some secret family recipe."

She set down her fork. "Um, I think Mom gets it from a deli over on San Pedro."

He took another bite and chewed thoughtfully. "It's delicious. It's all delicious."

"The secret to a good brisket is to take it slow." Joni's father spoke from the end of the long picnic table set up under an oak tree in the Montgomery back-yard. "You can't rush something this good."

Carter nodded. "I'll have to remember that." Good advice for briskets, and for relationships. He glanced at Joni again. She was studiously cutting her meat into tiny pieces, her cheeks flushed as if she'd had too much sun. *Ah, Joni, I don't want to rush you*, he thought. *I just want you to give me a chance.*

G.P. pushed aside her plate and surveyed her guests with a satisfied smile. "As soon as everyone's finished eating, we'll start the games."

The announcement was met with groans.

"Do we have to?"

"Aren't we too old for that?"

"I think I sprained my ankle."

"Nonsense," G.P. countered. "The games are a tra-dition at every family gathering."

Carter leaned across the table to whisper to Joni. "What kind of games is she talking about?"

Joni rolled her eyes. "Stupid ones. Kid stuff like three-legged races and balloon relays. She thinks they build closeness and togetherness."

"They keep you all from being too serious." G.P. directed her comment to her granddaughter. "I have very good hearing for a woman who's almost sev-enty," she added.

Carter shoved his chair back from the table. "Sounds like fun." He nodded to Joni. "Can I be part-ners with Joni?"

G.P. smiled. "But of course."

So half an hour later, Carter found himself standing hip to hip with Joni at one end of the backyard with her siblings, cousins, nieces and nephews paired up alongside them, ready to compete in a three-legged race. He slipped his arm around her and hugged her close. "This could be fun," he said.

She stared down at the pink ribbon that bound them together at the ankles. "I feel ridiculous."

"Actually, you feel very nice to me." He bumped his hip against hers. "Your grandmother's right. This togetherness thing is great."

"Don't get any ideas." Her voice was stern, but her eyes were filled with barely suppressed mirth.

He glanced along the starting line at the competition. "So what do you think our chances are?"

She craned her neck to follow his gaze. "Bruce and Peter won last year. The little kids generally fall apart giggling halfway across the yard. But Larry is pretty good. If he and Susan can stay together, they might have a chance."

He looked back at her. "Have I mentioned that I have this competitive streak? I hate to lose."

"Why doesn't that information surprise me?" She put her arm around him, hooking her fingers through the belt loop of his jeans. "I'm something of a sore loser myself."

"Is everybody ready?" G.P. climbed onto a folding chair in the middle of the yard and raised her arms. She beamed at the ragged line of contestants. "Ready. Set. Go!"

Carter leapt forward, dragging Joni along with him. "Hey, wait for me!" she cried. Wrapping both arms around him in an attempt to stay upright, they came to an abrupt halt.

"Sorry. This is harder than it looks." He checked the competition. "Damn. We're already way behind."

"If we want to win, we have to work together. Like this." She hugged him tight against her, pressing her thigh firmly against his. "Now when I say go, we take one step together."

"I could get used to this togetherness thing."

She rolled her eyes and said, "One, two, three, Go."

"Go. Go. Go." They fell into a hopping rhythm, covering ground at a surprisingly fast pace, passing everyone as they headed toward the length of surveyor's tape held by G.P. and the youngest Montgomery grandchild.

"Here come Joni and Carter, in first place. But Bruce and Peter are gaining fast. Who will be the winner?" Joni's father provided commentary from his perch in a lawn chair alongside the finish line.

"Go. Go. Go." Joni and Carter made a frantic dive for the tape, arriving inches ahead of her cousins, and collapsed into each other's arms.

"Did we win?" Carter gasped, rolling onto his side to face Joni. They were both breathless and laughing, still clinging together.

"I think we won." She smiled into his eyes, her previous shyness forgotten in the moment.

How was it you could be surrounded by other people and suddenly be so aware of one other person? He could feel her heart beating wildly against his chest, echoing the pounding of his own. Her hair had come undone and fallen across her forehead. He reached up to push it out of her eyes and left his hand there, cradling her cheek. She grew still, eyes still locked to his, her lips parted as if in silent invitation.

It would be so easy to lean down and kiss her....

"There'll be time for celebrating later, you two." G.P. stood over them, a grin splitting her face. "We've got more games to play."

She nudged Carter with her toe and he had no choice but to shove onto his knees and offer a hand to Joni. "What's the next challenge on the list?"

"Next we have the orange relay."

Joni groaned. "G.P., no!"

"What's the orange relay?" Carter asked.

"Oh, you'll see."

She started to walk away, but Carter pulled her back. "We're partners, remember?"

"You don't need a partner for this game."

"Then I need you to make sure I don't embarrass myself by not following the rules."

Joni shook her head. "The whole point of this game is to embarrass yourself."

"Everyone line up now." G.P. clapped her hands. "Form two lines, right in front of me. Ben, where are those oranges?"

Carter found himself in line between Cousin Larry and Joni. "The object of the game is to pass an orange down your line without using your hands," G.P. explained. "If you drop the orange, your team has to start over."

"This looks easy enough," Carter said.

Joni gave him a pitying look. "It's not."

The thing about an orange, he discovered, is that it is small, round, and surprisingly slippery. Studying the other players, he decided that the key to accomplishing the exchange was to flex your knees, relax your neck, and let the other person do most of the work.

Larry, for instance, was a pro. The two men were about the same height, which made it easier. With a minimum of fumbling, Carter had the orange under his chin, to the admiring applause of his team and worried glances from the competition.

Feeling confident, he turned to pass the fruit to Joni and immediately saw that anatomy was not on his side. For one thing, Joni was a good six inches shorter than he was—and considerably better endowed in the chest area. From this angle, he had a tantalizing view of her cleavage which was, to say the least, distracting.

"Hurry up," she prompted, and angled her neck up to take the fruit.

He bent to tuck the orange beneath her chin and found himself pressed against her breasts, much closer than he'd planned on getting with her entire family looking on.

He tried to back up a little and almost lost the orange. Laughter swelled around him. He glanced at Joni's face. Her perfectly calm expression seemed to indicate that none of this had the slightest effect on her. But the hard points of her breasts pressing into his chest made a liar out of her face. Joni was definitely aware of what was happening between them, and though she might never admit it out loud, she liked it.

The thought sent an extra zing of pleasure through him. Why not have a little fun with this? He shifted, deliberately rubbing against her. Her nipples made a delicious friction against the thin layers of fabric between them. He moved again, shimmying the full length of his torso against her in a subtle bump and grind. Oh yeah. He had the hang of this game now.

"What are you doing? Stop that!" she hissed.

"I'm trying to pass this orange to you." He raised his eyebrows in feigned innocence.

Talking was a mistake. As soon as he opened his mouth, the orange began slipping. He fought to keep hold of it, but the uncooperative fruit popped out and rolled down his chest.

He lunged for it, succeeding in capturing it before it hit the ground. Except that now he was bent over, his chin against the orange, which had lodged between Joni's breasts. His nose was buried in her throat, the scent of coconut sunscreen and orange making him think of hot Caribbean days and even hotter Caribbean nights.

It wasn't what you could call a comfortable position, but he figured he might as well enjoy it. He put his hands on Joni's hips and pulled her closer, to the delight of the crowd.

"We should have never let those two play," someone said. "They're enjoying it way too much."

"At the rate they're going, we'll never win," someone else added.

"Pass the damn orange," Joni ordered.

"I'm trying." He bent his neck, attempting to grab hold of the slippery fruit.

Joni's nipple was at eye level now, practically begging to be touched. He gritted his teeth and wished he hadn't worn jeans that were quite so tight.

With a grunt, he finally snagged the orange and carried it back up toward Joni's neck. She sighed and arched toward him, giving him an enticing view of her milk-white throat. Carter closed his eyes and reminded himself that now was not the time to be fantasizing about tracing his tongue along the curve of her neck.

Egged on by the calls of their teammates, he finally managed to hand over possession of the fruit. Joni turned to pass it to her sister-in-law, Pam.

Carter let out a deep breath and surreptitiously tried to adjust his jeans. What a way to make a good impression on a date's family—get a hard-on that wouldn't quit.

Despite the delay he and Joni had caused, and thanks to a fumble by the other team, the orange reached the end of Carter and Joni's line first. "All right!" Carter cheered and clapped, but fell silent when he saw the last person in line turn and start the fruit back in his direction once more.

"What's he doing?" Carter asked.

"You have to pass the orange back the way it came in order to win," Joni explained.

Great. He and Joni got to do their dirty dancing routine all over again. Not that he hadn't enjoyed it, but it would have been better without an audience.

This time it was his turn to stand still while she tried to maneuver the orange to him, to the accompaniment of hoots and catcalls from the rest of her family. She was blushing furiously by the time she successfully relinquished the fruit. And Carter was wondering if he'd ever again be able to look at a citrus fruit without breaking into a cold sweat.

AFTER JONI'S TEAM WAS declared the winner of the relay, all she wanted to do was find a shady spot and drain a cold drink. Or maybe she could dump the contents of the cooler on herself for an outdoor version of a cold shower. Anything to chill the fire Carter had started inside her. Honestly, what was it about him that got her so riled up?

She watched him exchange high fives with Larry. Any other man would have been mortified to be subjected to these childish games but Carter acted as if he was actually enjoying himself. G.P. would no doubt award him the day's Good Sport award and move him to the top of her list of perfect husbands for her favorite grandchild.

Except that Joni had no intention of marrying Carter or anyone else her grandmother chose for her. Going along with fruit relays and three-legged races in the name of family harmony was one thing. She drew the line at marrying a thrill seeker. So that meant no cops allowed.

G.P. climbed onto her chair once more and clapped to get their attention. "We have one more game," she said. "Something easier this time, but just as fun."

"I'm beginning to wonder about your grandmother's idea of fun." Carter leaned over and whispered in her ear, his breath tickling the hair at the back of her neck and sending a jolt of heat through her.

"Didn't I try to warn you?" She hugged her arms across her body, recalling the feel of him brushing against her. If G.P.'s next game called for any kind of physical contact, she was faking a headache and calling it quits. A woman could only take so much, even to please her grandmother.

"This year, we're going to play blindman's bluff," G.P. announced.

Joni looked at Carter. "That's a new one on me. Do you know how to play?"

He shook his head. "Maybe it's something like pin the tail on the donkey?"

That sounded tame enough. "I suppose I'll tough it

out and play," she said, "especially since it's the last one. There are never more than three."

"I'm impressed with how everyone goes along with these games to please your grandmother," he said.

"She's a special lady." She shrugged. "And I guess...even if they're silly, we really do have a lot of fun."

"I can tell. It's one of the things I like most about your family."

And they like you. But she couldn't tell him that. He might think she included herself in that sentiment. Not that she didn't like Carter, but she didn't *like* him. Not in the more intimate way he obviously wanted.

"All right, everyone. Listen up." Grandmother Pettigrew addressed them from the chair that served as her podium. "Here are the rules. The first person to be it is blindfolded and spun in a circle. The other players take seats in chairs scattered around the area and clap to indicate their position. The player finds a person and sits in his or her lap, then attempts to identify them by feel only. If they guess correctly, then that person is it."

Joni felt queasy. She took a step away from Carter. She had no intention of sitting in his lap and making a fool of herself any more than she already had today.

To her relief, G.P. selected Joni's ten-year-old second cousin, Zach, as the first contestant.

Zach was blindfolded and spun around. Carter took a seat near the picnic table and Joni deliberately chose a lawn chair across the yard from him. "All right now, everyone clap," G.P. ordered.

The boy walked in a crooked circle, arms out-stretched, until he bumped into Joni. She suppressed a giggle as he climbed on her knees and gingerly patted her hair. He smelled like strawberry Kool-Aid and backyard dirt. "I can tell it's a girl," he called.

"Maybe it's your uncle Larry with a wig," someone called.

Zach shook his head. "Uncle Larry doesn't smell this good."

More laughter. He traced his hand along Joni's face, his mouth twisted into a frown of concentration. Joni remembered baby-sitting him when he was an infant. She'd spent hours rocking and hugging him. He'd probably make a face if she did that now. "It isn't Mom because she's not wearing glasses," he said.

"That boy could be a detective someday," Carter said.

Zach patted her shoulders, then moved down her arms to her hands. He felt each finger. "No wedding ring," he said. He grinned. "I know who it is now."

"Who is it?" G.P. came to stand beside Joni's chair.

"It's cousin Joni!" Grinning, he pulled off the blindfold to the applause of everyone.

Joni managed to keep smiling. Great. Even her young cousin was clued in to her position as the family old maid.

"All right, Joni. Now it's your turn." G.P. held out the blindfold.

"And no fair choosing Carter," Bruce called.

"Yeah, we should make Carter sit this one out," Larry said.

Carter stood and moved behind his chair. "You're taking all the fun out of it for me."

Relieved that Carter had been eliminated, Joni allowed Zach to lead her to the center of the circle, where G.P. fastened the blindfold, the spun her around three times. "Everyone change places," G.P. called. "We don't want to make this too easy for her."

It took Joni a few seconds after she stopped turning to regain her balance. She shut her eyes tightly beneath the blindfold, trying to picture where she was standing in relation to the chairs. Previously, most of the adults had taken seats on the shady side of the circle, she recalled, while the younger family members had opted for the sunny side. Odds were the older family members weren't going to give up their shade. Her best bet would be to head for the sunny side and pick one of her young cousins, who could probably be identified by the sound of their giggles alone.

She began an awkward trek across the ground, stumbling from time to time, ignoring the catcalls of her older cousins. "Over here, Joni!" Someone—she thought it was Marcus—called in a falsetto.

"No, Joni sweetheart, here," answered his brother Larry.

When she felt the sun on her shoulders, she

stopped and reached out, instantly coming in contact with the arm of a lawn chair. Moving up a few inches, she felt a hand, one that was too large to belong to one of the children. She started to back away, but G.P.'s voice stopped her. "No, you have to stay with whoever you choose first."

She leaned forward to grope at her mysterious quarry's hair. "In the lap! In the lap!" came the cries.

Reluctantly, she eased onto the man's lap. Strong arms came around to help her settle on a pair of knees. It was definitely a man. Even Aunt Lisa didn't have arms that hairy.

She found her way to his hair again. It was thick, warmed by the sun and surprisingly soft. That eliminated her father and her brother Matt, who kept their bald pates covered with ball caps.

From the hair, she moved carefully, tracing one finger past his temple and down, trying to imagine the shape of his face. Whoever it was was keeping very still. She felt the muscles of his jaw tighten as she caressed him. He seemed to be barely breathing.

She stroked his cheeks. He was clean shaven. That knocked out Greg and Uncle Richard. But she felt definite beard stubble, which eliminated Zach's fifteen-year-old brother, Thomas, who could boast only peach fuzz above his lip.

She moved her hands out to his shoulders and smiled. Did Larry or Bruce have shoulders this nice? She smoothed her hands down his chest. He wore some kind of knit shirt with a collar, which didn't help. Half the men here today wore golf shirts.

"Who is it?" one of the women asked.

She shook her head. "I don't think it's Daddy, Matt, Greg or Richard. Probably not Bruce or Larry."

"Use all your five senses," G.P. advised.

She leaned closer and sniffed. Soap—familiar but not distinctive. A faint, not unpleasant hint of male sweat, not surprising since they'd all spent the afternoon playing in the hot sun. Smoke from the barbecue pits. But pretty much every man in the family had visited with her father as he cooked the brisket.

"Don't you know who it is?" Someone—she thought it was her mother—asked.

She shook her head. "It's not Thomas or Zach." She was running out of male family members. Who the hell was it? "Are you trying to trick me with someone I don't know?"

"It's someone very familiar to you," G.P. said.

She smoothed her hands down the man's arms and twined her fingers with his. No rings, but most of the men in her family didn't wear rings, even the married ones. Speaking of rings... She checked the ears. No earrings either, so it wasn't Bruce.

What else hadn't she examined? She hesitated, then slid her fingers around to brush his lips. Her breath caught and her heart beat faster. That was silly. Maybe a man's lips in general made her think about how she was sure Carter had been about to kiss her earlier.

"Come on, guess!" She was sure that voice belonged to Marcus. Unless he had hidden talents as a ventriloquist, that eliminated him from the list of possibilities.

"I can't believe you don't have better powers of observation than this," G.P. said.

Who else was left? She wracked her brain, trying to think of someone she hadn't already ruled out. She rested her hand on the man's chest. He didn't feel particularly hairy, but could she really tell through the shirt?

He was warm, strong. She'd imagined she'd feel awkward, sitting on his lap like this, with his arms around her. Instead, she felt comfortable. As if he'd welcome her to stay here all day.

She moved her hand over and felt the thump of his heart, strong and rapid. Her own heart rate increased at the sensation. He shifted beneath her and she became aware that he was aroused. She held her breath, afraid to move, even as heat coursed through her. Why was this man turned on? And why was *she* getting turned on by someone she couldn't even see?

She looked around, sending an accusing look through the blindfold in the direction she thought her grandmother was standing. Had G.P. played a trick on her? Had she made her think Carter wasn't participating in this round, then slipped him in as some kind of test for her?

And what did it mean that he was the one she'd selected, out of everyone in the circle?

It would be just like G.P. to do something like that. Just like the rest of the family to go along with the joke.

But what if it wasn't Carter? She turned her head to face the man again. If she guessed Carter, then took off this blindfold and found someone else in front of her, she'd embarrass herself, and possibly give away the charade she'd concocted to keep G.P. from meddling.

"Hurry up, we don't have all day," G.P. said. "Who do you think it is?"

"I think I know, but I want to check one more thing to be sure." She knew one sure way to induce her mystery man to give himself away. And if she was going to embarrass herself, she might as well go for broke.

She cupped her hands on either side of the man's face, then leaned forward and kissed him.

As soon as their lips touched, she knew. The man who had been as still and emotionless as a mannequin came to life beneath her, his arms encircling her more tightly, drawing her closer to him. She tilted her head to deepen the kiss, and sighed as he responded in kind. Her racing heart and roaring blood drowned out the catcalls and hoots from onlookers. Her body felt hot and liquid, every sense heightened.

She could blame the blindfold, which blocked her sight and made her more aware of every sensation. She could point to the incongruity of sitting on a man's lap in the middle of her parents' backyard, which made this kiss different from any other. But the part of her that refused to lie to herself knew the reason for these feelings was the man himself. From their first embrace in the parking lot, she had known Carter spoke to her body with an amazing, exciting, and sometimes frightening intensity.

She couldn't have said how long they sat there, kissing without shame while her entire family looked on. It was probably only a few minutes before she came to her senses and pulled away from him. He reached up and unfastened her blindfold, leaving her blinking at the sudden brightness, avoiding his gaze. She didn't want him to see how he had touched her, how easily she'd surrendered control to a man she scarcely knew.

She slid off his lap and brushed at her shorts, fighting the blush she couldn't keep from warming her face. "There's no fooling you, is there?" G.P. crowed, putting her arm around Joni's shoulder. "I should have known."

As gracefully as possible, Joni slipped out of G.P.'s grasp. "I'd better go see if Mama needs help in the kitchen," she said, and before anyone could protest, she took off across the yard, running from their laughter and good-natured teasing. Running away from her own crazy feelings.

4

INSTEAD OF SPENDING a lot of money on therapy, maybe more people should wash dishes, Joni thought as she stood before a sinkful of soapy water half an hour later. Swishing plates and cups through the warm water had such a calming effect, and the tang of lemon dish soap was as effective as any aromatherapy.

"I'm sure I could finish these myself if you want to go back out and visit with everyone." Her mother brought a stack of dessert plates to the counter. "Carter might think you've abandoned him."

"Carter will be fine." He struck her as a man who would be at home in any situation. And he'd certainly embraced her family. She supposed that came of having none of his own.

Maybe that explained his decision to become a cop, too. If you had nothing to lose, why not take a job where you regularly risked everything? Not that it mattered to her what he did with his life. After today and the one date she'd agreed to, she'd probably never see him again. She plunged her hands into the dishwater and scrubbed furiously at an already clean plate.

"What are you doing hiding in here?" G.P. swept into the room, her arms full of dirty glasses. She set the glasses on the counter and turned to Joni. "I want you and Carter to go shopping with me tomorrow." She grinned. "He already told me he doesn't have to work, and I know you're off, too."

Joni rinsed a handful or silverware, avoiding G.P.'s gaze. Her grandmother was up to something. But what? "Why do you want to take us shopping?"

"I want to buy you some nice things for your honeymoon."

"Honeymoon?" The knives and forks clattered in the sink as they slipped from her hand. She whirled to face G.P. "But we haven't—"

G.P. patted her hand. "You will soon. It's easy to see how much you and Carter care for one another. I predict wedding bells before long."

Of course, this was what Joni wanted her to think. Now G.P. wouldn't have to launch her own search for a man she thought suitable for her granddaughter. Still, she hadn't expected the charade to go so far as having them plan for a honeymoon. "That's really sweet of you, G.P.," she said, drying her hands on a dish towel. "But Carter and I don't need anything. And I hate to delay you when I know you're probably anxious to fly out to Charlotte for the air show."

"Don't be ridiculous. I've already let everyone know I won't be at the show this year, that I'll be spending time with my favorite grandchild." She took Joni's hand in hers and patted it. "So that's what

I intend to do. Besides, I'm looking forward to the opportunity to get to know Carter better. I want to make sure he's really the right man for you."

"Of course you do." Joni felt weak. She ought to know by now that no one could argue with G.P. and win.

As soon as the dishes were done, Joni went in search of Carter. The sun had set an hour ago, though the daytime heat still lingered. The younger cousins chased after fireflies in the darkened side yard, while their older relatives gathered lawn chairs under the trees and talked in low voices. The aromas of barbecue smoke and suntan oil mingled with the perfume of the roses that grew beside the back porch, calling forth memories of all the summer nights she had spent in this house. She and her girl cousins would gather at one end of the porch with their Barbie dolls and talk about boys and romance and the weddings they would one day have. Who would have guessed back then that finding true love would be so difficult?

She found Carter playing horseshoes with her father and her brother David under the glow of the mercury vapor light in the back corner of the yard. "He's beat me twice already," her dad said, sighting through the upturned ends of a brass horseshoe. "I told him we have to make it best three out of five."

"I think his strategy is to wear me out." Carter leaned against the fence, long legs stretched in front of him, eyes half-closed in a look that was more seductive than sleepy.

Joni looked away, pretending she hadn't noticed. "Can I borrow Carter for just a few minutes?" she asked.

Her dad straightened. "I suppose so." He tossed the horseshoe aside. "David, let's you and me go see if there's any ice cream left."

"We need to talk," Joni said when she and Carter were alone.

Carter's smile could have melted a whole freezer-ful of ice cream. "I thought maybe you wanted to kiss me again."

She crossed her arms and tried to look stern. "I didn't *want* to kiss you the first time. I was merely proving a point."

"If you want to believe that, you go right ahead." He straightened and walked toward her. "But I think the only point you proved was that you and I share a very powerful attraction." He stopped in front of her, his body angled toward her, so close she could see the shadow of his beard along his jawline, and the faint scar beside his lip. "There must be a reason for that, don't you think?" he said.

She swallowed, somehow finding her voice. "Unlike you, I don't believe everything happens for a reason. Maybe my reaction to you is merely hormonal, or due to some phase of the moon."

He laughed. "I think it's hormonal all right, but the moon has nothing to do with it."

She forced herself to turn her back on him. It was too difficult to concentrate when she was looking into his oh-so-serious eyes. "Have you heard G.P.'s latest plan?"

"You mean the shopping trip?"

She nodded. "Did she tell you she wants to buy us clothes for our honeymoon?"

"H-honeymoon?" His laughter drew stares from across the yard.

She whirled to face him again. "Shhh. You don't want to give people the wrong idea."

He touched her shoulder. "I thought that was what this was all about—giving people the wrong idea about us."

"G.P. certainly fell for it. She's already hearing wedding bells."

"Then mission accomplished. Why are you so worried?"

"I'm not sure. Except that G.P. always takes things too far. She was supposed to meet you, decide you were perfect for me, then head out of town. The longer she stays, the better the chance she'll find out we're a couple of frauds, and then I'll be back where I started."

"I promise I'll do my best not to make her suspicious." He smoothed his hand up and down her arm. "I'll be the perfect devoted boyfriend."

That's what I'm afraid of, she thought. She shrugged off his hand. "I suppose we'll have to keep pretending a little longer. With any luck, after tomorrow, G.P. will decide she's seen enough and decide to go home or to Charlotte, or wherever her next adventure takes her."

She started to turn away, but he caught her by both arms and held her fast. "Don't forget, once she's gone, you still owe me one date."

She nodded. The last thing she wanted was to date him, but she was a woman of her word. Besides, what could happen on one date?

Just as importantly, what could go wrong on one shopping trip with an almost seventy-year-old woman?

CARTER AVOIDED SHOPPING MALLS as much as possible. As far as he was concerned, the right way to shop was to have a specific objective in mind. Decide what you wanted, choose one store that carried the item, and get in and out as quickly as possible. You didn't compare prices, consider different colors or try anything on.

Women, on the other hand, looked at shopping as a form of entertainment. They actually spent whole days buying a single dress. They apparently enjoyed visiting multiple stores to look at very similar items, and discussed accessories and options the way some men discussed basketball scores. A man could buy a whole year's wardrobe and be back home opening a cold beer in the time it took a woman to choose five items she even wanted to try on.

So he couldn't say he was thrilled about spending the day cruising the mall with Joni's grandmother.

The fact that Joni would be along was the only saving grace. If he spent enough time with her, maybe she'd loosen up and stop denying her feelings for him.

"I want to visit my favorite boutique first," G.P. said as Carter guided the car into a parking place in the garage of North Star Mall. Famous for the giant pair of cowboy boots towering over the front entrance, North Star was also home to some of the most upscale shops in town. "Then we may need to visit Neiman's, Macy's, and a few other places."

"Just what exactly are you planning to buy?" Joni asked as she helped G.P. out of the car.

"I want to buy you several nice outfits." She settled her purse on her shoulder. "I'm not saying these clothes have to be for a honeymoon or anything, but they're the type of things a young woman might wear on a romantic holiday. And that could be a honeymoon, or not." She looked at Carter over the top of her sunglasses. "Not that I'm pressuring you or anything. Consider this humoring an old woman."

Carter grinned. "Consider yourself humored. I can think of worse ways to spend the day than escorting two lovely ladies."

G.P. nodded. "Then we'd better get started. We have a lot of ground to cover." She led the way toward the walkway that linked the garage with the mall.

Joni hurried to catch up with her. "Why do we need Carter here?" she asked. "I mean, wouldn't it be better to, um, surprise him…later, I mean?"

"That only applies to wedding gowns. I want to make sure the outfits I buy please Carter as well as you."

"Joni would look beautiful to me in anything."

Her expression went all soft and vulnerable for all of a second, before she shot him a stern look. "Aren't you the silver-tongued devil?"

"I'm absolutely sincere." He swept her with a lingering look that left little doubt how much he appreciated every square inch of what he saw—and how much he'd enjoy getting to know every part of her better. The flush that swept up her throat told him she'd gotten the message.

G.P. led them to a fancy boutique with a name Carter couldn't pronounce and likely wouldn't remember. One of those places where all the mannequins in the window look pissed off and the chairs are too fragile to sit on. "Madame Pettigrew, how nice to see you." A very tall, very thin woman with ink-black hair that looked as if it had been cut with a hedge trimmer took G.P. by both hands.

"Monette, this is my granddaughter, Joni, and her friend, Carter Sullivan. We're interested in seeing several outfits for Joni. Something suitable for a romantic getaway."

Monette nodded. "Where will you be going?"

Carter realized all three women were looking at him. He cleared his throat and glanced at Joni. Where would she like to go? Where would he like to take her? Someplace exotic. Sexy. Romantic. "We haven't exactly decided yet," he said. "But I'm thinking Tahiti."

Joni's eyes widened. G.P. clapped her hands. "Tahiti. How wonderfully romantic."

Monette smiled. "We have a number of outfits that would be most suitable." She led them to a kind of sitting room at the back of the store. "Wait here and I will bring a few.things for you to consider."

Carter sat between Joni and G.P. At least the sofa was comfortable, even if it was covered in pink brocade and so low to the ground his knees stuck up in front of his nose. The air smelled like flowers and the music playing in the background featured soaring violins and New Age birds and stuff. The whole place made him want to go hang out at an auto parts store or a bowling alley—anywhere to shake off this estrogen overload.

Monette reappeared, her arms laden with what looked like yards of brightly colored scarves, but turned out to be dresses and skirts and blouses and every other kind of feminine clothing imaginable. Carter had no interest in the clothes themselves, so he watched Joni.

She perched on the edge of the sofa cushion, her arms folded under her breasts, a dazed look on her face as the clerk presented outfit after outfit and extolled their virtues. "This is the latest fashion, very hot," Monette cooed as she draped a diaphanous skirt over Joni's arm.

Joni nodded, the lines of her mouth tightening and

her shoulders slumping further. Normally outspoken, she grew quieter and quieter with each new outfit added to the pile in front of her.

As the clerk and G.P. discussed the merits of silk over rayon, Carter leaned over to whisper to Joni. "What's wrong?"

Her eyes darted to his, then away. "What makes you think something's wrong?"

"You haven't said a word in ten minutes. That's the longest you've been silent since I've known you."

She flashed him an irritated look. He laughed. "That's better. You're not usually reluctant to express your opinion. What's the matter?"

She opened her mouth to answer, but G.P. interrupted. "What are you two whispering about over there?"

"Joni apparently isn't thrilled about something, but I can't tell if it's the clothes or Tahiti."

"Tahiti's fine." She uncrossed her arms and smoothed her hands down her thighs. "I've always wanted to go there."

"Then it's the clothes." He leaned over and fingered the edge of a blue-and-purple silk sarong. It felt soft, sensuous. "I don't know much about clothes but these look beautiful to me."

She shook her head. "They're not my style. They're too sexy. Too revealing."

"You have a beautiful body. You should show it off," G.P. said. "I'm sure Carter would agree."

He grinned. "I'm with you there, G.P."

"These clothes are designed to make a woman feel beautiful and sexy," Monette said. She flashed a smile at Carter. "To make a man desire her."

Joni's frown deepened.

"Why don't you try them on before you pass judgment?" G.P. said.

Reluctantly, Joni allowed Monette to lead her to the dressing rooms, leaving Carter alone with G.P.

"Even as a little girl, Joni was timid," G.P. said. "I don't mean a coward, but…reserved. I never understood that." She looked at him. "Do you?"

He considered the question. He felt the need to defend Joni, to protect her from anything remotely like criticism. "I think she's a person who guards her feelings," he said after a moment.

"Guards them too well." G.P. patted his hand. "You've been good for her. Already I can see you're helping her to come out of her shell. Even six months ago, she would never have kissed a man in front of us all the way she kissed you."

He shifted in his seat, remembering that kiss. He'd been dying, sitting there unable to move while she touched him all over. When she'd brought her lips to his, he'd lost control a little bit, returning the kiss despite the fact that they were far from alone.

She could say what she would about hormones and phases of the moon, but he knew their physical response to one another hinted at a stronger emotional connection worth investigating further. Besides, didn't it mean something that, even blindfolded, she'd chosen him out of a crowd? If that wasn't fate at work, what was it?

G.P. checked her watch. "She's been in there quite a while now. What could be taking her so long?" She leaned forward to look toward the front of the store. "I see Monette is with another customer. You'd better go and check on Joni. Make sure she's all right."

Carter stood, then hesitated. "I'm not sure I'd be welcome in the ladies' dressing room."

"Nonsense. There's no one else in there. And if there is, each room has its own door."

Glancing around to make sure no one could see him, he ducked behind the curtain that divided the dressing rooms from the rest of the store. It was easy enough to determine which one Joni occupied, as only one door was shut. He tapped on the door.

"Who is it?"

"It's me. G.P. sent me in here to check on you."

"I'm fine. It takes a while to try on this many out-fits."

"Have you found any you like?"

"I'm not sure."

Above the drone of violins, he heard voices approaching—the clerk and her other customer. "Let me unlock a dressing room for you...."

Great. She'd probably think he was some kind of pervert who got his jollies peeping at women in dressing rooms. He bent closer to the door. "Joni, let me in," he whispered.

"What? No, you can't come in here."

"Someone's coming. Let me in just until the coast is clear."

He thought at first she was going to ignore him. He looked around for somewhere else to hide, but there wasn't so much as a potted plant in the short, straight hallway. Then, just as the clerk appeared in the mirror at the end of the hallway, the doorknob rattled and the door swung open.

He darted in, slamming the door behind him, then leaned against the wall, stifling laughter. The first thing he noticed was how small the space was. Maybe six by six. And part of that was taken up by a bench on which Joni had stacked her purse and other clothing. The rest of the space was filled with hangers of clothes and a large mirror.

The next thing he noticed was Joni herself, cowering behind several dresses still on hangers. One bare shoulder peeked above a red-and-black silk skirt. He grinned and whispered, "Are you naked under there?"

"Of course I'm not naked," she hissed. Indignant, she pushed the hanging clothes aside. Carter sucked in his breath. She was dressed, but barely, in a pink-and-white bikini top and a short slit skirt. The bikini barely contained her full breasts, and the skirt hugged her hips and thighs, accentuating her curves.

"Carter? Carter, what's wrong? You've gone all white."

Probably because he'd forgotten to breathe. He

nodded to her. "That outfit...it's the kind of thing men fantasize about."

She glanced down. "No wonder. I'm practically naked." She contemplated the pile of discarded clothes on the bench. "The rest of these aren't much better. Blouses cut down to my navel or slit up to my crotch. Or else fabric so tight it leaves nothing to the imagination."

He picked up a strapless red dress. Imagining Joni wearing this brought a rush of heat straight to his groin. "I'll bet every one of these outfits looks great on you," he said.

She made a face.

"No! Don't be that way. You're beautiful." He took hold of her shoulders and turned her to face the mirror. "Look at yourself."

The woman looking back at them had everything a man would want in a partner: creamy skin, lush curves, shining hair. Carter could never get enough of looking at her.

Joni frowned. "My stomach is too big."

"No, it's not." He brought his hand around to rest on her stomach. She was soft, curved. Incredibly erotic. He swallowed, staring at his sun-browned skin against her pale perfection. "You look like a woman should look."

She was still frowning, seemingly oblivious to the effect she was having on him. She tugged at the bikini top. "I think this is too small."

He grinned. "I think it's supposed to be that way."

He moved both hands up to cup her breasts. "You know what they say—if you've got it, flaunt it."

She flushed and met his gaze in the mirror. "Carter, I really don't think..."

"Shhh." He stroked his thumbs along the sides of her breasts, watching in the mirror as her eyes lost their focus. Had any woman ever responded to his touch this way?

He traced lazy circles around her nipples and felt her tremble. She leaned back against him and he maneuvered her so her bottom cradled the fabric-covered ridge of his erection. One arm across her stomach, the other fondling her breasts, he bent and kissed her neck, flicking his tongue across her satin-soft skin.

She squirmed her bottom against him, and he had to bite his lip to keep from moaning out loud. What would she do if he suggested she turn around and relieve this frustration they both were feeling, right in front of the mirror?

The knocking on the door sounded loud as gunshots. They both froze, eyes wide with shock. "Is everything all right in there?" Monette asked.

"Y-yes. Everything's fine. I'm almost done."

"Let me know if you need anything in a different size or color."

"I'll do that."

When the clerk walked away, Joni elbowed him in the stomach, sending him back against the stack of dresses on hangers. "I think you're getting a little too into this whole pretend boyfriend thing," she said.

"So it's all my fault, is it?"

"I didn't say that." She sorted through the discarded garments until she found her own clothes. "I'm as guilty as you are, letting you take advantage of this meaningless physical attraction we have for each other."

"Who says it's meaningless?" He crossed his arms and watched as she replaced clothes on hangers. "If that's the case, why don't we just go for it?"

She glared at him. "What are you talking about?"

"If these feelings between us are meaningless, what's the harm of indulging ourselves and having a little fling? A purely physical relationship. No strings attached."

She shook her head and went back to sorting clothes. "You may be able to do something like that, but I have higher moral standards."

He moved closer, forcing her to back up against the mirror, though she kept a bundle of clothes between them. "So you're saying that for you to have a satisfying physical relationship, there has to be an emotional attachment as well?"

"That's exactly what I'm saying. And since you and I don't have that, I have no intention of going to bed with you."

He looked around at the clothes-strewn cubicle. "This isn't exactly bed."

She shoved him toward the door. "Out, so I can get dressed."

"Miss Montgomery, is there someone in there with you?" Monette's voice was higher-pitched now. Anxious.

Joni reached past Carter and undid the door lock, then opened the door and shoved him out. "My *boyfriend* was just helping me with a zipper," she said. "He's leaving now."

Carter nodded. "I'm going. But you won't always get rid of me so easily."

WHEN SHE WAS ALONE again, Joni sagged against the dressing room wall. Her skin still tingled with the memory of Carter's hands on her, and every nerve hummed with frustrated desire. The moment he'd entered the tiny cubicle, the air had been charged. She'd known she shouldn't let him put his hands on her, but the part of her that craved his touch was stronger than the part that told her it was a bad idea.

Annoyed to find her hands still shaking, she stripped off the bikini and skirt and reached for her clothes. But her own reflection in the mirror stopped her. What did Carter see that attracted him so? Though she didn't consider herself fat, she'd never had the thin, athletic figure that was the modern ideal. She had ample breasts and hips, and a small waist. What used to be called an hourglass figure.

The way a woman should look, he'd said. She flushed, remembering the heat in his eyes when he'd stared at her, the tenderness of his hands as he'd fondled her. The man did things to her, made her forget who she was and where she was and what she wanted for her future.

She didn't want a man like Carter, someone who lived so close to danger. But she had a hard time remembering that when she was with him. No matter how much she told herself he'd only hurt her, the warning vanished from her mind the moment his hands or his lips touched her.

The only solution was to avoid him as much as possible. G.P. would leave soon and after that they'd have one date and that would be it.

Clinging to this resolve, she dressed and gathered up the clothes. At the last minute, she set aside the bikini and skirt and the red dress. After all, if she didn't choose something, G.P. would make her stay here until she did.

G.P. stood to greet her. "I was hoping you'd come out here and model for me," she said.

Joni faked disappointment. "I'm sorry. I didn't know."

"Well, as long as you and Carter are pleased with your choices." She paid for the purchases and led the way out of the store. "Now for shoes."

Joni stifled a groan. At least shoes didn't require her to get naked, but she didn't have the strength to model ten different styles of sandals while Carter directed smoldering looks at her legs.

When she looked his way, she discovered he was

staring at her. He winked, then took G.P.'s arm. "Why don't we have some lunch first? I'm hungry."

Joni figured she owed him for the reprieve. *Thanks,* she mouthed. Now that the pressure was off, she realized she was hungry, too.

"What would you ladies like?" Carter asked when they reached the food court.

G.P. surveyed their choices. "I'll have a gyro," she said, nodding toward a Greek deli.

They waited in line at the deli, then carried their trays to a table by the center court fountain. "Whenever I eat Greek food, I'm reminded of the time George and I visited Greece. We hadn't been married very long when he got the chance to fly stunts in an air show there." She ate a bite of her gyro, then dabbed at the corners of her mouth with a paper napkin. "Have you ever flown in a small plane, Carter?"

He shook his head. "No, I haven't had the privilege."

"Oh, it's thrilling. George used to take me up with him sometimes. You feel so free when you're flying. So untethered and uninhibited. It's one of the things I miss most now that he's gone."

Joni's throat tightened. Whenever G.P. talked about Grandpa, her face glowed like a new bride. She had loved him so much. It hurt now to think of them not together. Did people still fall in love like that, so completely they went on loving after death?

G.P. leaned across the table and took Joni's hand. "Watching you two together, I remember all over again what it's like to fall in love." She reached for Carter's hand also. "Carter, I want you to come to dinner this weekend. Just the immediate family this time."

He nodded. "I'll be there."

She looked at Joni. "And I expect by then you two will have a special announcement to make."

5

BETWEEN WORRYING over what to do about G.P. and reliving every burning moment of her dressing-room encounter with Carter, Joni spent a miserable night. What was G.P. thinking, practically demanding an engagement announcement from the two of them? It was enough to send the typical boyfriend running for the hills. To Carter's credit, he'd played along with everything very smoothly.

Of course, Carter wasn't her typical boyfriend. And to her extreme frustration, her behavior was anything but typical around him. She'd spent years avoiding the daredevil type, looking for a sensible, safe man, only to find she was as physically vulnerable to a bad boy as any other woman she knew.

She clenched her thighs together as she lay in bed, remembering just how vulnerable. Once Carter's mouth and hands were on her, her common sense skipped town. Talk about taking risks—continuing to hang out with Carter was like juggling a lit fire-cracker. Sooner or later, she knew she was going to get burned. But what choice did she have, since G.P. had issued her ultimatum disguised as a dinner invitation?

When the alarm went off at six, she covered her head with the pillow and squeezed her eyes shut. Did she have enough money in her savings to buy a one-way ticket out of town, and out of the ridiculous mess her life had become?

Somehow she forced herself out of bed and made it to work on time, where the aftermath of a morning rush-hour traffic pileup effectively distracted her from her own problems. By the time the last of the accident victims was transferred to the Intensive Care Unit at about ten-thirty, she felt she'd reclaimed some of her sanity.

"Now who do you think is sending flowers to the E.R.?" Marcelle looked up from the computer screen and stared down the hallway. Marcelle had seen Joni's failure to hit it off with her cousin as Joni's loss and Joni had wisely agreed. Last she'd heard, Brian had recently asked out a nice young woman from his office. Someone, Marcelle had implied, with better taste than Joni.

"Maybe the delivery guy turned down the wrong hallway," Joni said, watching as what looked like an impressive arrangement of roses on legs moved toward them. "He's probably looking for the patient floors."

A man's head peered from around the roses. "Where can I find a Joni Montgomery?"

Marcelle stared at Joni, her eyes wide. Joni gasped. "Uh, that's me," she stammered.

"These are for you." The deliveryman shoved the

vase up onto the counter in front of her. "Haveanice-day," he muttered and left.

Joni stared at the flowers, heart pounding. She had a pretty good idea who had sent them and it wasn't fair. She could live with Carter being sexy and beloved by her family, but how could a woman stand her ground against a man who was all that, and romantic, too?

"Who are they from?" Marcelle stood and leaned in to sniff the wine-red blooms. "Aren't you going to read the card?"

Trying to ignore the crowd of coworkers and passersby who gathered around, Joni plucked the card from the plastic holder in the vase and opened it. "Thought you would enjoy these. Carter."

At least he hadn't tried to be cute or suggestive. She fingered one velvet-soft petal and leaned in to sniff the soft perfume. She couldn't even remember the last time anyone had sent her flowers.

Marcelle leaned around Joni to peek at the card. "I guess Brian couldn't compete with that," she said. "He's never been one to spend money foolishly."

Yes, roses were foolish. But they were also sweet. Joni hunted in her purse for the cell phone number Carter had given her and dialed it. He answered on the third ring. "Hello, Joni."

"How did you know it was me?"

"Who else is going to call me from Santa Rosa?"

"I wanted to thank you for the flowers."

"You didn't look too happy when I left you last night. I thought they'd cheer you up."

Cheer wasn't the word she would have used. After all, she still hadn't figured out what to do about G.P. or Carter. "They're beautiful," she said. "Thank you."

"You know we still need to talk about this weekend, don't you?"

She sighed. "I know. I have half a mind to just tell G.P. to butt out and leave us to make our own decisions about our relationship."

"All that will do is hurt her feelings. And it probably won't stop her."

"You're right." She stared at the roses. In the warmth of the room, some of the buds were already unfurling more.

"What time do you get lunch? I go off duty at eleven. I can pick you up and we can go somewhere to talk."

"No, really—" Talking on the phone was one thing, but she wasn't yet ready to see him in person.

"Come on. I know a great Mexican food place over on Naco Perrin."

Her stomach grumbled. The bowl of cereal she'd had for breakfast had long since vanished. And a public restaurant ought to be safe enough. "All right. I'll meet you out front at 11:45."

Carter was waiting for her when she emerged from the building shortly after 11:30. He was standing under the front portico with his back to her, dressed casually in boots, jeans, and a Texas Rangers T-shirt. Her heart beat faster and a smile automatically formed on her lips the moment she caught sight of him. She struggled to appear sober and unaffected before he turned around.

Then he turned and spotted her, and made no attempt to hide how glad he was to see her. He came to her and put his arms around her in a bear hug. His enthusiasm touched her, but also made her wary. "You don't have to pretend to be madly in love with me when my family's not around," she said, trying to sound as if she were making a joke.

"Who says I'm pretending?"

She looked away, unsure if he was teasing or not. After all, he'd made that crazy declaration in front of her family two days ago.

He drove southeast from the hospital and parked in the lot behind a storefront restaurant, *La Bonita*. Brightly colored greasepaint on the windows announced the daily specials: Fresh *menudo, tacos al carbon* and *carne asada*. Inside, a dozen tables shared space with a covered steam table and a small wooden bar. Paper flowers and Mexican flags decorated the ceiling and the aroma of garlic and peppers made Joni's mouth water.

"Officer Sullivan! So good to see you." A handsome older man in a *guayabera* shirt held his arms wide in greeting.

"Good to see you, too, Miguel. How are you doing?" Carter slapped the man on the back.

"*Bièn*. I have a table for you and your lovely lady here by the window." Miguel led them to a glass-topped wooden table. "Elena will be right over to take your order."

Joni tucked her purse underneath her chair and looked around at the other diners. A mix of laborers from nearby construction sites and suit-clad office workers filled every table and crowded along the bar. "Do you come here often?"

"It's part of the neighborhood I patrol, so I'm in here fairly often. They have the best *carne guisada*."

"That sounds good." They both ordered *carne guisada* tacos with guacamole. The waitress had barely departed when the front door opened and a very attractive young woman with waist-length blond hair, low-slung jeans and a ring in her navel burst into the room and headed for their table. "Carter! It's so good to see you!"

Carter stood and wrapped his arms around the blonde. "It's good to see you, girl. How are you doing?"

"I'm doing great." She moved back enough to get a good look at him, keeping one hand on his waist. "I work just down the street, at a clothing store. I was passing and saw you through the window and just had to say hello."

Joni fiddled with her teaspoon, trying not to notice Carter's hand on the blonde's hip, or her perfect perky figure. Was this an old girlfriend of his? She looked awfully young, but then some men...

"Joni, I'd like you to meet Tessa Phillips. Tessa, this is Joni Montgomery."

"Nice to meet you." Tessa offered her hand and Joni shook it.

Then they all stared at each other. Tessa and Carter still had their arms around each other while Joni debated what her reaction was supposed to be. "So how do you two know each other?" she asked after a moment.

"Carter just about saved my life." Tessa shoved both hands in the back pockets of her jeans. "When I met him I was so messed up, living on the streets. He helped me get it together and get my life back."

"You did all the work. I just pointed you in the right direction." Carter looked more like a proud father than an ex-boyfriend now.

"He's so modest." Tessa leaned toward Joni. "You know the first time I met him, I spat at him." Her eyes widened. "Can you believe that? To me he was just The Man, trying to hassle me. But even after that, he kept coming back, talking to me about how I had so much going for me if I'd just make an effort. He never gave up." She punched him playfully on the arm. "I never met anybody so stubborn."

"Hey, when I know what I want, I won't take no for an answer." But he was looking at Joni when he spoke, not Tessa.

Elena returned with a steaming plate in each hand and Tessa moved aside. "Hey, I'll let you eat now. It was good seeing you again." She waved to Joni. "Nice meeting you."

Joni concentrated on adding salsa and sour cream to her taco. "She seems like a really sweet girl," she said after a moment.

Carter spooned salsa onto his plate. "She is now. She wasn't very sweet when I met her."

"But you still helped her."

He shrugged. "You hang around the streets long enough, you learn to spot the kids who still have a chance to get out. She tried to act tough, but underneath you could see the hurt. She was only fifteen, too young and too pretty to last long if I didn't get her to straighten up."

Joni laid down her fork, too interested in this glimpse into Carter's life to eat. "What happened? I mean, why was she living on the street to begin with?"

"Old familiar story. Mom hooked up with a new boyfriend, boyfriend started hitting on her, mom took the guy's side. So she left. At first, she was hanging with some friends, then they ditched her and she hooked up with a boy. A loser who got her on drugs and threatened to beat her up if she didn't do what he said."

Joni's stomach clenched as she tried to imagine the healthy, pretty girl she'd just met as a homeless addict. It didn't seem possible the two people were the same. "How did you help her?"

Carter chewed and swallowed. "I convinced her to

go to a shelter, got her into a treatment program and a mentoring program. After that, it was up to her." He grinned. "You don't know how good it makes me feel to see her now."

His pleasure in Tessa's accomplishments touched her, but she wasn't ready for him to know. She picked up her fork again. "You really did save her life."

He shook his head. "I didn't do anything anybody else wouldn't have done, if they had connections to the resources I have."

But how many people would even bother to make those connections? How many times had she crossed the street to avoid coming into contact with any of the rough-looking teens who haunted the sidewalks and parks in certain parts of town? Carter took the time to stop and talk to them. To see them as real people.

The more she knew about him, the more the picture in her head labeled "cop" got distorted. She'd classified him as a daredevil danger seeker but now she had to add that he was a man who loved family, even though he had never really had one of his own. He was a man who reached out to kids who needed help. A romantic who believed in the power of fate to bring love into his life.

She could almost feel her resistance crumbling. What was happening here? She swirled a chip through a puddle of salsa on her plate. "I guess, being a cop, you never really leave the job behind," she said. "You can't really live a normal life."

"Who says I can't?" He put down his fork and

studied her. "We're having a normal lunch now, aren't we?"

She glanced around at the restaurant full of ordinary workers. "It looks that way, but we haven't been here half an hour and already two people have referred to you as 'Officer' Sullivan." She leaned forward, lowering her voice. "I'll bet you're even carrying a gun."

He frowned. "Then you'd lose that bet. I purposely left my off-duty weapon at home because I didn't want to freak you out." He slid his hand across the table to cover hers. "I know the fact that I'm a police officer makes you uneasy, but I'm asking you to give me a chance here."

She flushed and slid her hand away from him. She didn't know whether to be flattered or annoyed that he'd left his gun at home because of her. The weapon itself didn't bother her—just the fact that it was in his best interest to wear one. Ordinary men—accountants and shoe salesmen—didn't have to think about those things.

"About dinner with your family Friday night..."

His words reminded her of more immediate problems. "What are we going to do? I'm afraid if we go along with G.P. and pretend to be engaged, she'll insist on helping to plan the wedding."

"I think we should stall. Go to dinner, be perfectly nice, but make no announcement," he responded.

"What if she flat-out asks? I wouldn't put it past her."

He regarded her over the top of his iced tea glass. "I'll give her my most charming smile and say that true love has its own timetable and can't be rushed."

The romantic words, not to mention the heated smile, had her melting in her chair. It might even work on G.P. She was just about to say so when a woman's piercing voice interrupted them. Joni turned to see a middle-aged woman standing just inside the front door, looking around frantically. "Someone call the police!" the woman gasped.

"What is it?" Miguel rushed to help the woman to a chair. "What is going on?"

"There's a man out there breaking into a car." She pointed to the curb.

Carter already had his phone out, punching in 9-1-1. "Possible auto theft in progress at 2500 Naco Perrin, La Bonita Restaurant," he said as he headed toward the door.

"Where are you going?" Joni asked, following him.

"To check on the situation. You stay inside."

Joni had no intention of staying put, and wasn't surprised when Carter didn't even notice her following him out the door. In a split second, he'd transformed from a laughing softie to a grim-faced officer of the law. A man who put his job first, even when he was off duty.

Joni stared as a man in a black knit cap popped the lock on a blue Honda and groped under the dash. In the distance, Joni heard sirens. Were they headed this way? She moved to stand beside Carter. "What are you going to do?" she asked.

He shook his head. "Nothing right now. The cavalry's on the way."

She was about to congratulate him on his good sense when a woman ran toward them from across the street. "Get out of my car!" she screamed, and bashed the would-be thief in the face with her purse. Raining curses down on the man, she grabbed his collar and tried to pull him out of the car.

Carter muttered an expletive and started forward. The thief shook the woman off, then turned and punched her in the jaw and shoved her into the car. The engine roared to life.

Carter launched himself at the car. Before the thief could pull away from the curb, Carter jerked open the door and dragged the man from the driver's seat. The two men rolled onto the sidewalk, each grappling for control.

Joni opened her mouth to scream, but no sound emerged. She stared, horrified, as Carter and the man fought. The thief slammed his fist into Carter's eye, sending him reeling. Carter countered with a sickening punch on the thief's jaw, only to have his head snapped back by a fist to his cheek. The crowd cheered as if they were watching a wrestling match. "Go get him, Carter!" Miguel cried, punching at the air.

Carter rolled the thief onto his stomach and straddled him. Joni looked up the street. Why weren't the police here yet?

A gasp from the crowd made her look back in time to see that the thief was clutching a wrench he'd pulled from who knows where. Carter fumbled at the small of his back—searching, she realized in horror, for the gun that wasn't there. Joni only had time to scream before he brought the wrench up against the side of Carter's head with a sound like a hammer hitting a watermelon. Carter collapsed to the sidewalk, and the thief heaved himself up and took off running.

Joni didn't know how she reached Carter, but suddenly she was kneeling by his side, her hand to his bleeding head. "Carter, are you all right?"

He opened his eyes and blinked at her for several seconds before his vision focused. He tried to shove up onto his elbows, but she pushed him back down. "You're hurt. You shouldn't move."

He glared at her. "The bastard's getting away."

She glanced down the street and saw two uniformed officers cuffing a man in a black knit cap. "It's all right. They got him. Hold still." His face against the bright red blood was horribly pale. She swallowed against the sudden nausea that rose in her throat and tried to blot the blood with a paper napkin someone handed her. As a nurse, she knew it wasn't unusual for even minor head wounds to bleed profusely. It wasn't like her to be queasy at the sight of blood. Maybe it was because she hadn't really eaten much lunch.

The woman who owned the car loomed over them. "Is he going to be all right?"

"I'm fine," Carter grunted, though his voice sounded as if he were speaking from a long way off.

"I'm so glad." The woman clasped her hands together. "You saved my life."

"Just doing my job," he mumbled, closing his eyes.

"You're a hero." The woman turned to the crowd of spectators. "Isn't he a hero, folks?"

They applauded, then moved back as two paramedics rushed up. "We'll take over now," one of them said, pushing Joni gently away.

Someone helped her to her feet and she backed away, unable to look any longer at Carter's blood-covered face. She found her purse in the restaurant, threw some money on the table for their bill, then walked down the street and hailed a taxi to take her to the hospital. Once there, she couldn't bring herself to go in. Instead, she found her car, then drove to her apartment, where she called in sick.

"You sound terrible," her supervisor said. "What's wrong?"

"Just...a virus, maybe. I'm sure I'll be fine tomorrow."

She went into the bathroom to change and for the first time noticed the blood on the tunic of her scrubs. Carter's blood.

It had only been a wrench, but what if the car thief had had a gun? *Oh God, what if Carter had been killed?*

The realization knocked her to her knees. Her nausea returned and she retched into the toilet. Afterward, she leaned against the bathtub, trying to control her shaking. She hated feeling this way, hated caring so much about a man who regularly put his life on the line.

She could see today had been minor. What would it be like when he was in real danger, with people shooting at him, doing their best to kill him? She hugged herself, shivering. No way could she handle that. She refused to put herself through it.

She ought to be grateful this had happened now, before she let all her fantasies about what a sweet, romantic guy he was get the better of her common sense. She was smart to come to her senses now, before she did something stupid like let herself fall in love with him.

CARTER'S HEAD HURT where the thief had brained him with the wrench. His pride hurt knowing he'd done something so stupid as leaving his off-duty weapon at home. All because he'd been worried about upsetting Joni. He was lucky the dirtbag hadn't had a gun.

But mostly his heart hurt because he'd let Joni slip away yesterday. He'd tried calling her, but she refused to answer the phone. Obviously, the whole scene yesterday had scared her. He needed to explain that wasn't how things usually played out. He could count on the fingers of one hand the times in his career he'd actually drawn his weapon, much less come to physical blows.

Most of his job involved talking to people, filling out paperwork, and driving around trying to fight boredom. It wasn't all danger and excitement. When Joni understood that, she'd feel a lot better about him. About them.

He climbed the steps to her apartment and knocked on the door. No answer. But he knew she'd called in sick yesterday afternoon and today, and her car was in the parking lot. So that meant she was hiding.

He knocked again. "Come on, Joni. I know you're home. If you don't answer me, I'll stand out here and pound on the door until the neighbors complain."

"Go away."

"No." Tessa had said he was stubborn. Joni was about to find out how stubborn.

"I don't want to talk to you," she said.

"That doesn't solve anything. We have to get this sorted out. Don't forget we have dinner with your family Friday night."

"I'll tell G.P. you're sick."

"What's that going to accomplish? She'll be rushing you over to my place with a pot of chicken soup. Your grandmother doesn't strike me as the type of woman who's easily put off."

"I'll call you later."

"We need to talk now." He leaned against the door, lowering his voice. "Please, Joni. All this shouting is making my head hurt."

His blatant plea for sympathy was rewarded by the

sound of locks turning. The door opened a few inches, though Joni kept the chain on. "How is your head?" she asked.

"Four stitches. Want to see?" He angled his scalp toward her.

She looked away. "I'm glad you're okay."

"Can I come in, please?" He reached behind him for the basket he'd set on the railing. "I brought you something."

Her eyes widened. "Oranges?"

He looked down at the cellophane-wrapped basket of fruit. "They reminded me of you." He could still remember the feel of her breast against his cheek as he'd tried to maneuver the orange during the game at her parents' house.

She shut the door partway and released the chain, then stepped back and held it open. "You can come in."

Joni's apartment was a lot like her—not a lot of fussy frills, but definitely feminine. The furniture was white leather, the only artwork a single Georgia O'Keefe print hung over the sofa. A purple chenille throw draped across an armchair added a spot of color and softness.

"Thank you for the oranges." Joni set the basket of fruit on the bar that separated her kitchen and dining areas. She wore a pink T-shirt and shorts. The thin fabric of the shirt molded to her breasts, revealing that she wore no bra. She was barefoot, her hair loose around her shoulders. "What happened after I left?" she asked.

"The loser who hit me was hauled into jail. Had a list of priors as long as my arm. But you don't figure anybody is too bright who'll break into a car in broad daylight in front of a restaurant full of people."

She leaned back against the bar, her expression guarded, revealing nothing. "If you hadn't been there, he might have gotten away. And taken that woman with him."

He moved over to stand next to her. "She wasn't too bright either, attacking a man twice her size."

"What about you?" She gestured to his head.

He touched the jagged row of stitches. "I'm not too bright either, going after that guy without considering he might have had a gun, and I was unarmed." The thought still made him lightheaded if he dwelled on it too long.

She hugged her arms across her chest. "And you left your gun at home because of me." She shook her head. "Don't do me any more favors like that."

"I won't." He studied her a moment, his gaze searching. "I think the biggest mistake I made yesterday was not giving you enough credit for being an intelligent woman who could separate what a man does from what he is."

"What do you mean?"

He slid down the bar, until his elbow almost brushed her side. She tried to move away, but the wall was at her back. "I mean I'm a man who happens to be a cop. But that's not my entire identity. Whether I'm carrying a gun or not, I'm still Carter Sullivan—a man like any other man. With a man's thoughts and feelings." Thoughts and feelings about *her*.

She looked away from him. "Not every man goes around saving women, like you did yesterday. That makes at least two, if you count Tessa." She looked more unhappy than ever. "You must have quite a track record."

He frowned. "I'm not in this to be a hero."

She looked directly at him for the first time since he'd shown up at her door. Her eyes were dark and angry. "I think you are. You'd have to have a little bit of a superhero mentality to even take the job."

"I could say the same for you, you know."

She blinked. "What do you mean?"

"You're a nurse, right?" He leaned toward her. The scent of oranges in the basket mingled with her vanilla perfume. "You work in the emergency room. You spend every day saving people's lives."

"It's not the same. People aren't trying to kill me."

"They aren't trying to kill me either, most of the time. I spend most of my day on paperwork and driving around, being a 'presence' in the neighborhood."

She faked wide-eyed amazement. "The bad guys must tremble in fear when they see you coming."

"Right now I could care less about the bad guys. I want to know about *you*." He moved closer, so that his elbow brushed the side of her breast. "Do I make you tremble?"

She turned away from him. "Don't be ridiculous."

"Is it ridiculous?" He reached around and cupped her chin in his hand, and gently turned her to face him once more. "Because I think the real reason you try to avoid me is the way I make you feel."

Anger flashed in her eyes and crackled in her voice. "We've already established that I'm physically attracted to you. So what?" Every muscle tensed, as if she were on the verge of violence—or great passion.

Carter slid his hand down to rest against her throat. Her pulse beat against his palm, strong and rapid. "I give you more credit than that," he said, his voice almost a whisper. "Your body doesn't operate independently from your mind. If you're reacting physically to me, then it's because something in your head is turned on, too."

She continued to glare at him, arms hugged tightly across her chest. "So you can read my mind now?"

He brought his other hand up to cradle her head for a moment, then slid both hands out to her shoulders. Her folded arms pressed against his chest, a barrier keeping them apart. "Why did you run away yesterday? I want the truth."

She compressed her lips together and drew in a ragged breath. "I...I was upset. We were sitting there, having a perfectly nice lunch, and then you have to run out on me and put your life in danger for no reason at all."

He kneaded her shoulders, wishing she'd move her damn arms so that he could get closer. "You're saying I should have let that guy drive off with that woman in the car?"

"The cops were on the way. They would have captured him."

"Maybe. Maybe not. It's not a choice I wanted to live with." A choice she ought to understand. What if it had been *her* in that car?

"That doesn't mean I have to live with it, too."

His hands stilled. "You're afraid."

"No! That's not it at all."

"Yes, it is." He almost smiled. Why hadn't he realized this before? "You're afraid to get involved with a man who takes risks. You're afraid you might get hurt."

"That's not being a coward. That's being smart."

"So it's smart to deny yourself the very thing you want, all because it's safe. You'd rather feel nothing than feel too much."

She bowed her head, letting her hair fall across her face, hiding her expression.

He leaned in and kissed her neck, his lips resting against her skin as he spoke. "Do I make you tremble? Because you sure as hell shake up my world." He moved up, feathering kisses along her jaw, until he was hovering over her mouth. "You've got me thinking about things...wanting things...I haven't dared think about before." He pulled her closer, crushing her to him, heedless of her arms still locked between them. He kissed the side of her mouth, and then her lips, nipping, licking, suckling, lavishing attention on her sensitive mouth. "I want you," he whispered. "And I'm not going to let you pretend anymore that you don't want me."

She let out a gasp that was almost a sob and brought her hands around to cling to him. "Yes," she whispered.

"Yes what?"

"Yes, I want you, dammit!"

6

CARTER WAS RIGHT, Joni told herself. She was a coward. She'd been so terrified—not of the thief or the gun or any fear for herself, but terrified for Carter. One moment she was beginning to think that here was the man who might break her "no daredevils" rule, and the next he was lying at her feet, bleeding. He'd come so close to death. Too close. Her worst fear had almost come true right before her eyes. What woman wouldn't run from that?

When he'd shown up at her door she'd been weak-kneed with relief to see that he *was* all right. She'd told herself that as long as she knew he was safe, she could find the strength to tell him she couldn't see him anymore. This whole charade had been a bad idea, one she had known from the first would only bring her trouble and heartache.

But he was so stubborn! He wouldn't take no for an answer. Wouldn't even try to understand her point of view. He kept talking to her, touching her, kissing her, until she couldn't think. Couldn't do anything but feel.

All the terror and relief rushed back, mingled into this great wanting. Carter was alive. He was here.

Why was she wasting time arguing when they could be savoring all the things they had almost lost?

"I want you, dammit." The words drained away the last of her resolve, so that all she could do was cling to him.

He pressed her up against the wall, his body covering hers, his mouth on hers. They kissed deeply, tongues tangling, lips demanding. Her hands caressed his back, his arms, his butt. She couldn't get enough of touching him, tasting him. Every brush of his lips, every sweep of his tongue, reassured her that he was really here, and that he was all right.

She pressed herself against him, relishing the feel of his body against hers—the muscled plane of his chest, the smooth firmness of his stomach, the hot hardness of his arousal. He felt strong, invincible. As if nothing could ever harm him.

She brought one leg up over his hip, wanting to be closer. He grasped her bottom and pulled her tight against him. She arched toward him, trying to bring her hot, aching center closer still. She felt stretched taut by desire, fulfillment just out of reach.

He caressed her breast through the thin T-shirt, shaping his hand to her, dragging his palm across her sensitive nipple. She bit her lip but could not hold back a low moan. She had wanted this for so long.

He lowered his head to take her nipple into his mouth, every flick of his tongue sending tremors of arousal through her. Only his hand cupped under her bottom and the wall at her back kept her from sliding to the floor.

He transferred his attention to her other breast and the combination of heat from his mouth on one side and the air-conditioning cooling across the damp fabric on the other side almost sent her over the edge. She strained against him, grinding her pelvis against his erection.

He raised his head and looked at her, his eyes dark with arousal. "Maybe we should go into the bedroom," he said, his voice husky with need.

"I...I don't know if I can walk."

He put his other arm under her bottom, and bending his knees slightly, hefted her over one shoulder. "Hold on," he said and started across the room.

She laughed at his caveman approach, then her laughter changed to a gasp as his hand slid beneath her shorts, his fingers caressing her bare buttock. "Which is the bedroom?" he asked.

"F-first door on the right."

The room was dark, a single shaft of light underneath the blinds stretching across the end of the unmade bed. He pushed back the tangled blankets and gently lowered her to the mattress.

She lay back, staring up at him as he loomed over her, trying to catch his breath. He seemed bigger from this angle, taller and stronger. He might have been intimidating if she hadn't noticed the way his hair was mussed where she'd raked her hands through it, a square of white bandage showing through.

"How's your head?" she asked.

"What head?" he grinned.

She followed his gaze down, to the fly of his trousers, strained by his erection. Smiling, she rose up on her knees and reached for the button at his waistband.

While she fumbled with button and zipper, he caressed her back, her bottom, her thighs. "You feel so good," he said. He slid one finger under the edge of her shorts, around her thigh to her crotch. "You're soaking wet," he murmured.

Her answer was a low moan as he plunged his finger into her. She tightened around him, at the same time his zipper parted and his erection, still covered by his briefs, filled her hand.

He was hot and heavy, pulsing with need. She squeezed his length gently, then slid down to lightly scratch his balls with the tips of her fingers. She was rewarded with a groan, and the flicking of his thumb across the hardened bud of her arousal.

Then his hand was clamped around her wrist, pulling her away. "Let's take it a little slower," he said. "After all, we've got all night."

CARTER HAD NO INTENTION of taking all night, but if he didn't get her hands off him for a minute, things were going to be over before they started. And he wanted this to be good.

Leaving Joni on the bed, he went around the room, turning on lamps until soft light banished the gray shadows. The last lamp was on the dresser across from the bed, and when he looked in the mirror, he could see Joni watching him. She was propped on her elbows, her hair falling around her shoulder in sexy disarray. Her face was flushed with desire, her lips swollen from his kisses. He swallowed hard as a new wave of wanting shook him. "What are you doing?" she asked.

"I wanted to be able to see you better." He turned toward her again, stopping at the end of the bed. How much longer could he linger, when all he wanted to do was see her naked and writhing beneath him?

"Take your clothes off."

He blinked. "What did you say?"

She wet her lips. "Take your clothes off. I want to see you, too. All of you."

His skin felt hot, his hands clumsy as he fumbled for the tail of his shirt. Aware of her gaze burning into him, he pulled off the shirt and reached for his shoes. He hoped she didn't expect a sexy striptease. He didn't have the patience for that. Not now.

Since his pants were already undone, it was a matter of a single movement to get rid of them. He stripped off the briefs, too, and he was naked before her.

She sat with half-closed eyes, watching him while pretending not to watch. But the rosy flush across her cheeks told her he had seen all of him, and that she liked what she saw.

He knelt on the bed beside her. "Your turn."

She didn't protest when he tugged at her T-shirt, and obligingly sat up and raised her arms over her head so that he could strip it from her. She kept her arms up, her breasts thrust toward him, swaying gently.

He cradled her breasts in his palms, savoring the weight and heat of them. He brushed his thumb across her distended nipples and she sighed, a ragged exhalation of breath. He loved how her breasts were so sensitive, so responsive to his touch.

Reluctantly, he moved his hands lower to the waistband of her shorts. He unfastened the row of buttons at her fly, then tugged the shorts down her hips, revealing white satin bikinis trimmed in pink bows.

"What are you smiling about?"

He hadn't even realized he'd been smiling. He slipped one finger under the edge of her panties, right beside one bow. "Pink bows. They sound so innocent, but because of where they are, they aren't really."

She arched toward him, her hipbone pressing against his hand. "Take them off," she whispered.

"I don't know. I kind of like them on." He slid down until he was lying between her legs, his mouth hovering over her sex. He could smell the musk of her arousal, see the shadow of the brush of hair between her legs beneath the white silk. She stretched her legs alongside him, thighs splaying, opening to him.

We'd like to send you 2 FREE BOOKS
and a surprise gift to introduce you to Harlequin Temptation®. Accept our special offer today and
Live the emotion™

HOW TO QUALIFY:

1. With a coin, carefully scratch off the silver area on the card at right to see what we have for you—**2 FREE BOOKS** and a **FREE GIFT**—ALL YOURS! ALL **FREE**!

2. Send back the card and you'll receive two brand-new Harlequin Temptation® novels. These books have a cover price of $4.25 each in the U.S. and $4.99 each in Canada, but they are yours to keep absolutely free!

3. There's no catch. You're under no obligation to buy anything. We charge nothing—ZERO—for your first shipment and you don't have to make any minimum number of purchases—not even one!

4. The fact is, thousands of readers enjoy receiving books by mail from the Harlequin Reader Service® Program. They enjoy the convenience of home delivery...they like getting the best new novels at discount prices, BEFORE they're available in stores...and they love their *Heart to Heart* subscriber newsletter featuring author news, horoscopes, recipes, book reviews and much more!

5. We hope that after receiving your free books you'll want to remain a subscriber. But the choice is yours—to continue or cancel, any time at all. So why not take us up on our invitation with no risk of any kind. You'll be glad you did!

GET A *Free* MYSTERY GIFT...
We can't tell you what it is...but we're sure you'll like it! A FREE gift just for giving the Harlequin Reader Service® Program a try!

Visit us online at
www.eHarlequin.com

Your FREE Gifts include:

- 2 Harlequin Temptation® books!
- An exciting mystery gift!

HARLEQUIN®
Live the emotion™

Scratch off the silver area to see what the Harlequin Reader Service® Program has for you.

YES! I have scratched off the silver area above. Please send me the 2 FREE BOOKS and gift for which I qualify. I understand I am under no obligation to purchase any books, as explained on the back and on the opposite page.

342 HDL DU4C   142 HDL DU4S

FIRST NAME	LAST NAME

ADDRESS

APT.#	CITY

STATE/PROV.	ZIP/POSTAL CODE

(H-T-07/03)

THE HARLEQUIN READER SERVICE® PROGRAM—Here's how it works:

Accepting your 2 free books and mystery gift places you under no obligation to buy anything. You may keep the books and gift and return the shipping statement marked "cancel." If you do not cancel, about a month later we'll send you 4 additional books and bill you just $3.57 each in the U.S., or $4.24 each in Canada, plus 25¢ shipping and handling per book and applicable taxes if any.* That's the complete price and — compared to cover prices of $4.25 in the U.S. and $4.99 in Canada — it's quite a bargain! You may cancel at any time, but if you choose to continue, every month we'll send you 4 more books, which you may either purchase at the discount price or return to us and cancel your subscription.

*Terms and prices subject to change without notice. Sales tax applicable in N.Y. Canadian residents will be charged applicable provincial taxes and GST.

If offer card is missing write to: Harlequin Reader Service, 3010 Walden Ave., P.O. Box 1867, Buffalo NY 14240-1867

DETACH AND MAIL CARD TODAY!

BUSINESS REPLY MAIL
FIRST-CLASS MAIL   PERMIT NO. 717-003   BUFFALO, NY

POSTAGE WILL BE PAID BY ADDRESSEE

HARLEQUIN READER SERVICE
3010 WALDEN AVE
PO BOX 1867
BUFFALO NY 14240-9952

NO POSTAGE
NECESSARY
IF MAILED
IN THE
UNITED STATES

He covered her with his mouth, stroking her through the silk, one hand caressing her legs, his thumb stroking the silken skin at the very top of her thigh. He forced himself to go slowly, to give her every moment of pleasure he could. She wouldn't listen to him when he tried to tell her his feelings, but she wouldn't be able to stop listening and experiencing and knowing him now. This was his chance to tell her all the things with his body that she didn't want to hear from his lips.

He moved aside the thin band of damp silk and began to stroke her naked arousal with his tongue while he slid two fingers into her. She moaned and bucked against him. She was close now. So close.

When he moved away, she reached for him, but he stilled her, keeping his hands on her. "Shhh. Not yet. But I promise, not long now." He stripped off her panties, then stretched alongside her, pressing his body to hers, waiting for another bit of control to return to him.

"Please tell me you brought a condom with you," she said.

He grinned. "I brought one." Several actually. He'd known exactly what he had in mind when he came over here this afternoon and hadn't expected to leave disappointed.

"Good. Because if you hadn't, I would have had to kill you."

Laughing, he slipped off the bed and removed one condom from the pocket of his pants, then returned to her, tucking the foil packet under the pillow for safe-keeping. He lay beside her once more and brought his hand down to caress between her legs. "I'm sure if I'd forgotten, we would have thought of something."

Her answer was an incoherent murmur, and the insistent arching of her hips. He teased her nipple between his teeth and tongue while his fingers stroked and fondled her sex. His erection pulsed against her thigh as she jerked at his touch.

He increased his pace, feeling the tension in both their bodies building. He raised his head to watch her face, and saw her features tense, then release as her climax overtook her. Her long keening cry sounded like a shout of triumph to his ears, and the tremors that shook her traveled through him, too.

He retrieved the condom from beneath the pillow and rolled it on with shaking hands. The time for taking things slow had passed. He'd been waiting for this moment since the first evening they'd met—maybe longer.

As he moved over her, she spread her legs wider, opening to him. Her muscles tightened as he entered her, making him groan with pleasure. They moved in a steady, strong rhythm, each stroke building to the next, their hands caressing, stroking, reassuring. He closed his eyes and gave himself up to the moment. The feel of the woman beneath him, her hands caressing his back, the golden light against his eyelids, the scent of sex and vanilla, the sensation of blood rushing and heart pounding—they all collided in a shattering climax that tore a shout from his throat and left him gasping for air in the echoing silence.

They lay for a long time afterward, clinging to each other, saying nothing. He couldn't put words to the feelings tangled up somewhere between his head and his heart, but gradually one clear thought emerged: If he had ever doubted she was meant for him, those doubts were now erased. Joni Montgomery was the woman he'd been looking for all his life. From the moment he'd seen her reflection in his wineglass, he'd known.

If only he could convince her that he was the man meant for her.

JONI DIDN'T WANT to open her eyes. Opening her eyes would mean letting in the real world and putting an end to this incredible fantasy she and Carter had created. How else could she describe what had just happened between them? She'd never known sex to be such an incredible physical and, yes, spiritual experience.

And she didn't dare tell Carter.

The thought was like a dash of cold water, forcing her to open her eyes and stare up at the ceiling. No, she couldn't share her thoughts with Carter. He'd take them as proof that his whole "fated to be together" theory was valid.

She knew better than that. Great sex did not a lifetime commitment make, especially when so many other things in their relationship were wrong. They would never see eye to eye on his job, so what was the point of taking this any further?

"What are you thinking?" He stroked her cheek, the callouses on his fingers rough against her skin.

She turned to look at him, nuzzling her head into his palm. He had the sleepy look of a man well satisfied, eyelids at half mast, a half smile teasing his lips. Her stomach quivered, remembering the tenderness with which he'd touched her, and she felt her own lips curve in an answering smile. "Oh...nothing. I wasn't thinking about anything, really."

Five minutes after a man had just given you the most incredible orgasm of your life didn't seem the right time to tell him you never wanted to see him again.

Of course, it wasn't true that she never wanted to see him again. She just didn't want him getting any ideas that they had a future together. A short-term relationship—a few laughs, some great sex, a friendship—all those things were possible. But she wasn't going to spend the rest of her life with a man who would leave her sick with fear every time he walked out the door to go to work.

"What are you looking at?" he asked.

She realized she'd been staring at him for the last several minutes, as if trying to memorize a face she truly might not see again. She brushed her hand alongside his mouth. "Where did you get this scar?" Had someone shot him? Or had he been in a terrible fight?

He grinned. "Do you think it makes me look tough?"

Before she could answer, he laughed. "That's what the nurse told me when they were stitching it up. I was eleven years old at the time, so tough was a good thing to me."

"You were eleven?" So much for being shot. "What happened?"

"I was playing football with a bunch of other kids in the trailer park where I was living at the time. I went back to catch a pass and wasn't paying attention to where I was going. Next thing I know, I've run smack dab into the end of one of the trailers. Gashed my face open on a piece of metal."

"Oh no." She feathered her fingers over the scar, as if it might still hurt. "Your parents must have been horrified."

Too late she remembered Carter didn't have parents. Or did he? She realized she didn't know how old he'd been when he'd gone into foster care.

Her mistake didn't seem to upset him. "My foster mother was more worried I might bleed on her new rug. A neighbor actually took me to the emergency room." He shrugged. "When it was time for the stitches to come out, I was already living in another home."

"Where was your mom? Your real mom?"

He rearranged the blanket around them. "She was in and out of hospitals. She'd had a nervous breakdown, a drinking problem. She never could get it together."

"How horrible." Joni spoke around a knot in her throat. Her own family, as aggravating as they could be at times, had been there to support her at every milestone and through every crisis. She couldn't imagine having to go through life without them.

He smoothed his hand across her stomach. "It used to bother me, then I realized I could either let the past make me miserable, or get over it. I decided I preferred to get over it."

He made it sound so easy, but could a person really "get over" the wounds of the past?

"About yesterday..." he said.

"I don't want to talk about it." She suddenly didn't want to talk at all. She didn't want to think about the future, or saying goodbye, or anything but right here, right now, with this man. What they had couldn't last, but she intended to enjoy it while she could.

She rolled to him and stretched up to kiss the scar. She laid a trail of kisses from there to the white square of bandage that covered the new stitches. Her lips moved on, across his broad forehead, down his cheek, to the other side of his mouth. He had a terrific mouth, sensitive and skilled, able to give her so much pleasure.

She could lie here all night, just kissing him, but already the tension within her was building, her body demanding more than just kisses.

"Did you bring another condom?" she asked.

He grinned. "Several more."

"Several?" She didn't try to hide her surprise.

"I figured once we got going, we might not want to stop."

She kissed him, hard. "When do you have to be at work?"

"Not until tomorrow."

"Me neither. Maybe we can find something to do with all that spare time and a few condoms."

"Five."

"Five?" Her eyes widened. "Are you sure?"

He cupped his hand around her buttock and pulled her closer, until she felt his erection against her thigh. "Oh yeah. I'm sure."

7

JONI DECIDED she would rather have a root canal while being forced to listen to the Muzak version of the Bee Gees' greatest hits than sit through Friday night's dinner with Carter and her family. Her parents and G.P. would be watching her every move for some sign of impending nuptials. Meanwhile she'd be avoiding looking at Carter, afraid she might give away the fact that while she wasn't in love with him, she was definitely in lust.

The man in question looked particularly luscious tonight in a tailored black suit and white collarless shirt. She was wearing a demure blue dress with long sleeves and high collar, but any hope it might help cool things off between them was quelled the moment she opened the door to Carter. The slow drift of his gaze from her head to her toes turned her knees to jelly. "You look hot," he growled.

"Um, so do you."

She took a step back, but that only made him take a step forward. "Too bad we can't stay here and have dessert first."

"My mom gets very upset if her roast dries out."

He faked a dramatic sigh. "Then we'd better get

going." He offered his arm. "But you owe me dessert later."

"We'll see." An evening being interrogated by G.P. might be enough to quell any man's ardor.

When they arrived, her mother greeted them at the door, bypassing Joni to envelop Carter in a hug. "We read in the paper about your accident. I'm so glad you're okay."

"My accident?" Carter gave Joni a questioning look. She shrugged.

"She means your bust-up with that car thief." Her father came into the room. "Del, that was no accident. The man was doing his job."

"The paper called you a hero." G.P. joined them, putting her arm around Joni. "I'll bet you were so proud."

Joni stared at her shoes. Angry, upset, even terrified, but not particularly proud, no.

Carter slipped his arm around her waist. "Joni was with me when it happened. I think it shook her up a little."

She guessed that was the diplomatic way to describe her feelings. Furious didn't have quite the same ring to it.

"But everything worked out all right, didn't it?" G.P. said.

"I'm fine." Carter took his arm from around her and followed her into the living room. "It was really no big deal."

"You're too modest," Joni's mother insisted. She

perched on the arm of Joni's father's chair, and G.P. settled into a rocker. That left the sofa for Joni and Carter. He sat uncomfortably close to her, his thigh touching hers. How was she supposed to talk coherently when he was so close, the memory of their lovemaking so fresh?

"Don't they make a cute couple?" Joni's mother said.

"They're perfect for each other." G.P. nodded. "I couldn't have picked a better man for Joni myself."

Well, that was the point, wasn't it? Ten minutes after meeting Carter, Joni had known her grandmother would adore him. Even though he was the complete opposite of anyone she'd have picked for herself, she'd thought passing him off as her boyfriend would be a sure way to make G.P. back off. In hindsight, she'd have done better to pick a man who wasn't quite so sexy. It was tough to be sensible and platonic when a man was messing with your hormones.

"Is dinner ready yet, Mama?" she asked. "I'm starved." She glanced at Carter.

"Oh yeah, I'm hungry, too." Carter said the right words, but the look he directed at her made her think pot roast wasn't what he had in mind.

"Then let's eat." Her father stood and led the way into the dining room. Joni faltered on the way to her chair. Her mother had set the table with her wedding china, and the good silver, which usually only came out of their protective wrappings at Christmas, Easter, and the occasional very special occasion.

"Is something wrong?" Carter whispered to her.

She shook her head. Nothing was wrong except she was about to disappoint the people she loved most in the world. They wanted an engagement announcement. Romance. Happily ever after. And Joni didn't have any of that to give them.

"Then sit down." Carter nudged the back of her legs with the chair he'd been holding for her.

She sat, and somehow managed to force a pleasant smile to her face. This was her punishment for trying to pull a fast one on G.P. She'd have to sit here and take it like a woman.

"I hope you like pot roast," her mother said as she set a platter in the center of the table. Perfect potatoes, carrots and onions surrounded the beautifully browned roast.

"I love pot roast." Carter unfolded his napkin and laid it across his lap. "This looks delicious."

"You said you met Joni in a restaurant," G.P. said. "What were you eating?"

He grinned. "To tell you the truth, I was so taken with Joni, I can't even remember what was on my plate."

"It's true love when a man can't remember food," her father said as he carved the roast.

"I think it's so romantic," her mom sighed as she passed a bowl of gravy.

"Romantic meetings run in our family, you know," G.P. said.

"They do?" Carter passed his plate for a slice of roast.

"Oh yes!" Her mom leaned toward them. "Joni's father and I met at a serviceman's club when he was stationed at Kelly Air Force Base. We were both with other people, but we ended up dancing with each other all night." She looked at her husband, her expression tender. "It was love at first sight. After that night, we were inseparable. Three months later, we eloped."

"Same for me and Joni's grandfather," G.P. said. "The first time I saw him in his leather flight jacket, I knew he was the one for me." She chuckled. "Of course, he thought I was just some kid from the sticks. I was barely seventeen, and skinny. I didn't have much of a figure, and him being a pilot and from out of town, he attracted the attention of plenty of local beauties. So I knew I had to get his attention somehow."

Carter grinned. "What did you do?"

"I stowed away on his plane. It was a Stearman 4E—an open cockpit biplane. He was using the front seat to store extra gear, so I climbed down in there and pulled stuff over me. I was a lot smaller back then, but still it was an awfully tight fit, and I had to bite my tongue to keep from screaming when we took off." She laughed. "You have to remember, I'd never been up in a plane before and I wasn't expecting my stomach to end up in my throat."

"When did he discover you?" Carter asked.

"I waited until we were at altitude and I popped up in the seat. I had this smart introduction all planned, but the minute I looked around me, I was so thrilled all my clever words flew right out of my head. 'I can't believe you get to do something this exciting every day,' I said."

"Tell them what he said," Mom encouraged, as if everyone but Carter hadn't already heard the story at least fifty times.

"After he got over the shock of finding me there, he said, 'I've carried some pretty interesting cargo before, but I never met a woman who had guts enough to come up here with me.' G.P.'s expression grew dreamy. "I think he knew then that he'd met his match."

"And six weeks later, they were married," Mom said. She looked at Joni. "I guess it doesn't take the women in our family long to fall in love. When we find the right man, we know it's meant to be."

Joni wanted to sink down in her chair and throw her napkin over her head, the way she'd done when she was a little girl and wanted to disappear. How had she ended up in a family of such sentimental romantics?

"Joni told me when we first met that she didn't believe in fate bringing two people together."

She glared at the man next to her. Now she wanted to use her napkin to gag him. Or maybe make a noose...

"I don't see how she can say that now that she's met you," Mom said.

Carter grinned. "She's just a little bit stubborn, you know." He winked at her. "But then, so am I."

How was it one little flirtatious wink could have her stomach fluttering like a girl at her first dance? She was supposed to be angry at him. Why couldn't her body and her mind get together on her feelings about this man?

G.P. laid aside her knife and fork and looked at them. "Do you two have anything you want to announce tonight?"

Carter looked at Joni. She faked a smile and folded her napkin in her lap. "The hospital has instituted a new training program and I've been asked to be one of the instructors. It could mean a big raise for me."

Her parents and G.P. glanced at each other, their smiles faltering. In fact, G.P. gave up smiling altogether. "I wasn't referring to your job. Don't you have something else to tell us? Carter?" She speared him with her gaze.

To his credit, he didn't wilt under her stare. He shook his head. "No, G.P. But when we do, you'll be the first to know."

In the silence that followed, Joni imagined she could hear the gravy congealing. "Why don't we go into the living room for coffee and dessert?" Her mother broke the tension at last. "I made Italian cream cake."

Joni suppressed a groan. Homemade Italian cream

cake was another sign that this evening had been marked as a special occasion. She'd bet money there was a bottle of champagne chilling in the refrigerator, too.

Her mother refused all offers of help with the dishes, so Joni, Carter, her father and G.P. dutifully filed into the living room. G.P. sat in the rocker again, hands on her knees, and began to rock furiously, her gaze focused on her hands. Her wedding band still glowed there, the gold burnished smooth by over fifty years of wear.

Mom arrived with a tray of cake slices and cups of coffee. Carter took a bite and rolled his eyes in an expression of ecstasy. "Mrs. Montgomery, this is the best cake I have ever eaten," he announced.

Mom flushed and looked pleased. "I'm so glad you like it. But you must call me Del. After all, you're practically one of the family."

Joni managed to keep from spewing a mouthful of cake across the room. She lunged for her cup of coffee and took a scalding swallow. What were her parents thinking? If she and Carter were seriously involved, he probably would have fled the room screaming by now.

They managed to get through the rest of the dessert without any more embarrassing hints from her family. Joni was beginning to think she might just survive the rest of the night when G.P. set down her coffee cup and cleared her throat. "I have something I want to give you two," she said.

Joni stiffened. *Please let it not be some family heirloom or embarrassingly romantic keepsake.*

G.P. rose from her chair and handed Joni a red envelope. Joni turned it over in her hand. "What is it?"

"Open it and see."

Carter leaned over to watch as she slit open the envelope. She unfolded the card inside and stared at the engraved lettering.

"What is it?" Mom moved to the edge of her seat.

Joni cleared her throat. "It's a gift certificate for dance lessons."

"Exactly." G.P. returned to her rocker with the grace of a queen who had just bestowed a priceless gift on her subjects.

Joni frowned. "But G.P.—"

"No buts, dear. You didn't think I knew about all the times you skipped dance class to go to the zoo, did you?" She looked at her granddaughter over the top of her glasses. "I'm smarter than you think. I don't miss much."

Joni looked at the card again, her stomach knotting. This seemed innocent enough, but she knew better. "But why are you giving me these now?"

"They're for the two of you. I want to see you dance at your wedding, and to do that you need lessons."

"But—" Carter's hand around her wrist cut off her protest.

"Thank you, G.P.," he said. "It's a very thoughtful gift. I know we'll enjoy them."

G.P. nodded. "You'll see that she goes with you?"

He slipped his arm around her, pulling her close. Though she hated to admit it, she welcomed the support. Maybe because they weren't his family, Carter was able to handle her relatives so much better than she could. "I know we're going to enjoy dancing together," he said.

He was probably right, Joni thought. She would enjoy dancing with Carter. The trick would be to keep from enjoying it too much.

JONI SPENT the next eighteen hours trying not to think about Carter. Except for the few hours she managed to sleep, she failed miserably. Ever since he'd left her at her door the night before, he'd been intruding on her thoughts. Now that she was at work, she wasn't doing much better. The E.R. was having a slow morning. Joni was supposed to be catching up on paperwork, but how could she concentrate on government regulations when a sexy man had commandeered her thoughts?

She was grateful for the midmorning phone call that pulled her away from her paperwork, until she heard Carter's voice on the other end of the line. "Our first dance lesson is Thursday evening," he announced.

She leaned against the desk, her back to her coworkers. "You didn't have to go to all that trouble. I would have scheduled the lessons."

"Except that you would have put the lesson off as long as possible. Am I right?"

She sighed. "You're right. But what's the hurry? G.P. can't stay in San Antonio forever. The Tucson air show is in two weeks and she never misses that one."

"Not even in the name of romance?" he teased.

She gripped the phone tighter. "Not even for that. Despite the high value my family places on sappy sentimentality."

"Except you."

"Except me. That gene didn't get passed along."

"You never know. Maybe it hasn't had the opportunity to assert itself yet." His voice was low, setting every nerve on red alert.

"You only say that because you're such a romantic yourself," she chided.

"Guilty as charged. Or maybe it's the company I'm keeping. There's something about a sexy, beautiful woman that brings out my mushy side. When can I see you again? Naked."

His voice was turning *her* to mush. "I don't think we ought to go there again, Carter. The other afternoon was—"

"Incredible? Fantastic? Life altering?"

All of those and more. Which was exactly why she needed to avoid a repeat performance. "We were both emotionally vulnerable. We'd had a trying day. We—"

"Stop making excuses. The bottom line is I made

you scream and now you're all nervous because you lost control."

Her nipples tightened at the memory and she felt a corresponding tension between her legs. How was it possible for a man to turn her on using only his voice on the phone? She struggled to keep her own voice from betraying her emotions. "We're supposed to be *pretending* to have a relationship, remember? Sleeping together makes things too complicated."

"That's the point—we do have a relationship now. There's no going back. It may not be the romantic union your family thinks it is, but we've made a connection. Don't lie to yourself or to me. I think we owe it to ourselves to explore this further."

"Dr. Carmichael, report to the E.R., STAT," the hospital operator's voice blared over the loudspeaker. Why was the hospital's top trauma surgeon being summoned to the emergency department at this time of day?

"Dr. Gains, Dr. Ranja, report to the E.R. Drs. Carmichael, Gains and Ranja, to the E.R., STAT."

"Look, I can't talk about this now," Joni said. "I have to get back to work."

"Fine. But we have to talk about it later."

She hung up the phone and slumped against the desk. Yes, she and Carter had made a connection. A physical connection that left her aching for him when they were apart. But what was the point of continuing to go to bed with him? He wasn't the kind of man she wanted to spend the rest of her life with.

She just had to hang on until G.P. gave up and left town. Then her life could get back to normal, without Carter Sullivan turning things upside down.

Marcelle rushed by, pushing a loaded crash cart. "Better get ready. Things are about to get exciting around here," she said.

"Why? What's going on?" Joni followed Marcelle toward the first treatment room.

"We just got a call that they're bringing in a cop with a gunshot wound, *and* the guy who shot him."

Joni felt the floor tilt and grabbed hold of the wall for support. Her first thought was of Carter. But she'd just been talking to him. Surely it couldn't be him—

A siren's wail announced the arrival of an ambulance. Red lights bounced off the double doors leading to the loading ramp, then the doors burst open and two paramedics wheeled in a stretcher. An array of tubes, lines, and an oxygen mask almost obscured the patient, but Joni could make out the light blue pants and dark blue shirt of a San Antonio police officer. Relief surged through her when she was close enough to reassure herself it wasn't Carter lying there.

She immediately felt guilty. The man lying there was hurt, and it was her job to help see that he survived with as few complications as possible.

The E.R. physician for the day, a serious young intern named Dr. Trang, rushed forward to consult with one of the paramedics. As part of the trauma team, Joni took her place alongside the patient.

"Ready? One, two, three." At the doctor's command, the team lifted and transferred the patient from the stretcher to a gurney. The paramedics wheeled the stretcher out while the team went to work on the patient.

While Marcelle cut the uniform away from the officer's prone body, Joni ducked under the mass of outstretched arms and snaking tubes to draw several tubes of blood for matching. She concentrated on finding the vein and inserting the needle before she let herself look at the man's face.

He was younger than Carter, clean shaven and ashy skinned in the harsh fluorescent light. He was conscious, moaning softly and watching them with a dazed expression. "What's your name?" she asked. It was probably on the chart somewhere, but talking sometimes helped distract patients. And it let them know you saw them as a person, not a collection of maladies.

"Curtis." His voice was weak and raspy. "John Curtis."

"Where's your vest, Officer Curtis?" The surgeon, Dr. Carmichael, joined Dr. Trang and gingerly probed at the wound on the right side of John Curtis's chest.

Curtis sucked in his breath as Carmichael probed deeper. The shadow of a beard stood out against the papery whiteness of his skin. "I was stupid, thought I could get by without it today. Wasn't supposed to be on patrol."

"Bet you'll think differently next time."

Joni made a mental note to ask Carter whether he wore his vest, no matter what.

Dr. Carmichael laid a hand on Curtis's other shoulder. "You're going to be fine. Damn sore for a while, but you're a lucky man today."

"Yes, sir." Curtis looked at Joni and she gave him what she hoped was an encouraging smile. Did Carter know this man? Did they work together? She didn't have time to dwell on these thoughts. Already, the second ambulance was pulling up, carrying the young drug dealer who had shot the officer.

"B.P.'s dropping. Ninety-two over sixty-five," Dr. Trang said. "He's getting shocky."

"We'll have to put in a chest tube." Glancing at the blood pressure monitor, Dr. Carmichael made a small incision between the officer's two ribs and fed a plastic tube into the chest. Blood and air spurted through the tube and within seconds, the patient's blood pressure began to rise. "Let's get him up to surgery." Dr. Carmichael stripped off his latex gloves and tossed them in a nearby trash can, then reached for another pair. "The man who did this is here, too?"

"Right back here," Marcelle led the way to the second gurney that had just been wheeled in. "Multiple GSW, left thigh."

The next hour was a blur of activity as the E.R. team worked on the assailant and transferred him to the patient care floor. Joni's supervisor tapped her on her shoulder. "Why don't you take a break? You look all in."

She felt all in, though that was ridiculous, considering she dealt with worse trauma on a daily basis. She usually thrived on the excitement of the emergency department. No doubt she was worn out today from her lack of sleep the night before.

She went to the break room and poured a cup of coffee from the pot kept going twenty-four hours a day, then sat at the table and stared at the box of donuts that was delivered every morning by one of the hospital auxiliary volunteers. The donuts reminded her of being in this same room with Carter while he challenged her to admit her attraction to him.

On the phone today, he'd challenged her again, telling her not to lie to herself. All right then, she wouldn't lie. Yes, he touched her physically. And emotionally. But in the wrong way. If the sight of a wounded police officer she didn't even know could upset her so much, what would she do when it was Carter lying on that gurney? Granted, that might never happen, but it *could*. The possibility of him being hurt on the job was astronomically higher than that of a man who was, for example, a car salesman or an accountant.

She rose from the table and dumped the stale donuts in the trash. She would go to dance class with Carter. She would play out the rest of this charade for her family. But she would not get involved with a man who had the potential to hurt her so much.

8

Angela's Academy of Dance was located in a non-descript shopping center on San Antonio's north side. The sign out front advertised "Tap, Ballet, Swing, Ballroom and Country Western dancing for all ages."

"What kind of dancing are we signed up for?" Joni asked as Carter led the way across the parking lot.

"I doubt she'd have registered us for tap or ballet, and when was the last time you saw country line dancing at a wedding reception?"

"A couple of months ago? This is Texas. Anything's possible."

He laughed and held the door open for her. "I'm pretty sure it's ballroom dancing for us."

She frowned. "All those fancy steps look complicated. I'm liable to stomp all over your toes."

He winked at her. "Did anyone ever tell you you're cute when you're nervous?"

She stuck her tongue out at him and he laughed. He owed G.P. for finding one more excuse for him to spend time with Joni. He needed every chance he could get to break through her prickly defenses and prove she could trust her heart with him.

The dance studio consisted of a small reception

area and a large, high-ceilinged room. Track lighting overhead beamed down on a polished wooden floor. The mirrored back wall reflected the six couples and one instructor gathered for the lesson.

A forty-something woman in a leotard and long skirt greeted them. "Hello, I'm Angela."

"I'm Carter Sullivan and this is Joni Montgomery. We signed up for the class tonight."

Angela looked delighted. "Oh, the lovebirds! Welcome."

Joni nudged him. "What did you tell them?" she whispered.

"Nothing. I swear."

"When your grandmother called, she explained this was her gift to you so that you could learn to dance at your wedding," Angela said.

At least two of the female halves of the other couples said "Awwww," while their men frowned at him. *Sure, make us look like unromantic slobs,* their stares seemed to say.

Angela clapped her hands together. "Now that everyone is here, we can get started. First I want to welcome you to class. Whatever your reasons for being here tonight, you should be congratulated for taking the first step toward discovering the special world of dance."

The couples arranged themselves in a line in front of her. Carter rested his hand on the small of Joni's back, enjoying the chance to touch her, knowing she wouldn't move away.

"As we go through the steps of the various dances we'll learn over the next few weeks, I want you to approach them as if you were learning a foreign language," Angela said. "Dance is a language all its own. The various steps and movements express a wide variety of emotions, from anger to passion to love." She smiled at Carter and Joni.

"While many people prefer to begin with the waltz, I prefer to start with something more exciting. Something fun and exotic and sexy." She pressed a button on a portable stereo and lively percussive music filled the air.

"Can anyone tell me what kind of dance this music would be appropriate for?"

"Rumba?" someone guessed.

"No, but you're close."

"The tango," Carter said.

She nodded to him. "Yes, this is a tango, the first dance we will learn.

"The tango originated in Argentina in the latter part of the nineteenth century. It is known for its fluid, expressive movements. Some people consider it the most romantic of all dances, which is one reason I've chosen it for tonight." As the music continued to play, she motioned to Carter. "Will you be my partner to demonstrate for a moment?"

He joined her at the front of the room. "With any dance, but especially the tango, the man's job is to lead his partner in the steps of the dance. In the language of the tango, this is referred to as caring for your partner." She took Carter's hands and arranged his right hand on her upper back, and pressed the palm of her right hand into his left hand. "It is your job, gentlemen, to care for your partner and make the dance a beautiful, romantic experience for her."

She smiled at them. "Now remember—if you can walk, you can tango. The basic step in the tango is a walk. The man moves forward, the woman moves backward, always remembering to be in balance with one another and to move gracefully." She and Carter demonstrated this walk while Angela counted their steps. When they had reached the end of the room she looked up at him. "You have danced before?"

He nodded. "But my...uh, Joni hasn't danced much."

"You could have given her a private lesson."

"We thought learning like this, in a group, might be better." Left alone, he doubted he and Joni would do much dancing. At least not the vertical kind.

"The next step you need to know is the tango close. The man steps forward, the woman steps backward, they step to the side, then drag their free foot in. So it's like this—forward step, side step, draw." She and Carter demonstrated this in combination with the walk. Next, they demonstrated the lunging dip, or *corte*, one of the signature moves of the tango. "Let's practice these three movements," she said, stopping the music. "First the walk, then the tango close, then the *corte*. Then we'll put them all together."

She sent Carter to rejoin Joni. "Did you get all that?" he asked her.

She rolled her eyes. "Oh sure. You're going to wish you'd worn steel-toed boots."

A new song began and Carter faced Joni and took her hand. "Remember, all you have to do is relax and follow me." He led off with his right foot, forcing her to move her left foot back. Awkward step by awkward step, they advanced across the room.

"Relax." He shook her hand. "You're too stiff."

"This is a lot harder than it looks." She stared down at her feet, grimacing.

"Look at me," Carter instructed. When she didn't comply, he put his hand beneath her chin and forced it up until she was looking into his eyes. "Forget about what your feet are doing. Feel the music and follow me."

"A-all right. I'll try."

They began to move again, tentatively at first, then with more confidence. Carter kept his gaze locked to hers, losing himself in the seductive rhythm of the music and the sapphire depths of her eyes. He saw the moment the spell of the dance caught her. She relaxed in his arms and began to really enjoy herself. He shifted to bring her closer, until a scant inch of space separated them.

"You are all doing so well, I want us to add more movements to the dance." Angela chose another man as her partner and demonstrated the promenade and the tango cross.

"Now you try," she said, releasing the man.

Carter pulled Joni closer still, until their bodies were plastered together, his right leg thrusting between her thighs with each step forward. "Carter, remember we're in public," she whispered.

"Didn't you hear what she said? The tango is all about passion."

"That's right." Angela chose that moment to stand by them. "Everyone, it's all right to move closer," she said. "Latin dance is the language of love. Of desire."

BEFORE CLASS, Joni had worried about dancing backward, and about dancing in high heels. She'd been afraid she'd step on Carter's toes, or trip and fall on her face. She had never considered that dancing with Carter would be such a turn-on. How was she supposed to learn about *cortes* and promenades when every nerve in her body hummed with awareness of him and the merest brush of his arm against the side of her breast made her gasp and arch toward him?

Despite all of this, or perhaps because of it, she was enjoying the dance. She felt more confident than she ever had on the dance floor. She had Carter to thank for that, she knew. Just as he knew how to touch her in bed, he knew how to touch her on the dance floor.

The song ended and, reluctantly, she moved out of his arms. Angela talked about some mistakes she had seen and advised how to correct them. Joni only half listened, her attention drawn to Carter.

For a big man, he was graceful. Light on his feet.

When they danced, she felt light as well, as if he could pick her up easily and carry her to safety should danger arise.

She felt *cared for*, just as Angela had said. It was something she hadn't felt, something she hadn't particularly *wanted* to feel, since she was a little girl. What did it mean that she felt that way now with Carter?

Angela announced it was time for a break and the couples wandered out into the reception area, to the water cooler and the rest rooms. A couple of men stepped outside to smoke.

"Are you having a good time?" Carter asked.

She nodded. "Yes, I am. I didn't think I would, but I am."

Another couple approached, a petite blonde with glasses and a man with a brown goatee. They introduced themselves as Bonnie and Alan. "We're engaged also," she said. "We're getting married in two weeks."

"Congratulations," Joni said. The woman sounded so excited, so in love. When she looked at her future husband, her eyes took on a dreamy expression, though he was a thin, unassuming man with an uneven haircut and narrow shoulders.

"When is your wedding?" Bonnie asked.

"Uh, well..." Her cheeks felt hot as she struggled for an answer.

Carter came to the rescue. "We haven't set a date yet. We both have difficult schedules."

"That can be a problem," Bonnie agreed. "Al and I have changed dates three times. Things kept coming up at work and—"

"What kind of work do you do?" Carter asked.

"I'm a teacher and Al is an accountant."

Joni looked at Al again. This was the sort of man she'd always pictured herself marrying—someone nice and unassuming, with a safe, boring job. Yet looking at him now, she couldn't muster the least bit of attraction to him.

She winced inwardly. Was she really so shallow? A relationship had to have more going for it that just sex, didn't it? But what kind of relationship did you have without it?

Bonnie and Al moved on, leaving Joni alone with Carter once more. "Where did you learn to dance so well?" she asked.

"In high school I had a crush on the dance teacher's daughter, so I signed up for class. I didn't realize I'd be the only boy there. The other guys teased me so much, I considered dropping out. Then I realized as the only boy, I got to dance with all the girls. I figured I had the sweetest setup in the whole school."

"So you've always been a ladies' man?"

He laughed. "Not really. Frankly, I got tired of the whole dating scene. Even when I had plenty of women to go out with, none of them felt like a good fit." His eyes met hers. "Until now."

She looked away. What did he expect her to say? She didn't want to think too much about her feelings for him. Tonight, all she wanted was to relax and enjoy the moment.

"All right, everyone, it's time to get back to our lesson." Angela ushered them back into the studio and put on a new CD. "I want you to practice some more, but this time experiment a little. Don't be afraid to combine moves, to get a little adventurous, even a little naughty. Remember, this is supposed to be fun."

The throbbing beat of the music seemed to rise up from the floor, through the soles of Joni's shoes, echoing the pounding of her heart. The temperature in the room rose with the hot Latin rhythms, and she felt a fine sheen of perspiration at her throat, and a deeper heat where Carter's hands touched her.

The shuffling steps of the dancers made whispering sounds beneath the music, and the dizzying whirl of their reflections in the mirror made her feel as if they were in a dance hall full of people. She closed her eyes and felt Carter's hands on her tighten. The soft fabric of his trousers brushed her skin and his leg thrust forward. The muscles of her thighs tightened in response.

"Remember, dancing is a language without words," Angela said. "Your movements should say how you feel."

What was Carter trying to tell her with his movements? What did her body want to tell him?

Dancing like this was a little like making love with her clothes on, every sensation heightened by the knowledge that she was in a public place, and anyone might be watching.

When the music stopped, Angela smiled and put her hand on Joni's shoulder. "You are a natural," she said.

Joni blushed. The only dancing she'd done before consisted of standing a few feet from her partner, swaying and moving her arms, or, if the song was a slow one, standing close together, swaying and not moving her arms. "I guess I owe it to having the right partner," she said. Carter squeezed her arm, but she couldn't bring herself to look at him. Not yet. If she looked at him now, he would see all her confusing feelings for him.

"I want you all to go home and practice what you've learned tonight," Angela said. "I'll see you next week."

They filed out into the humid heat of the parking lot. Carter opened the car door for her. "It's early yet. Why don't we go back to my place? We can practice."

Practice what? But didn't she already know the answer to that? Common sense told her to turn down his invitation, but she was too on edge, too needy, to listen to common sense anymore. Tonight, she didn't want to go to bed alone. If that meant risking complicating her relationship with Carter even more, so be it. A woman could only be strong so long, especially when the alternative was lonely frustration.

"Yes, let's go practice our dancing," she said and settled back in the seat.

Neither of them said anything on the drive to his apartment. Joni was thankful for the silence, wanting to savor all the feelings the dance had brought forth in her—this wonderful, agonizing arousal, and this magical feeling of being so cared for.

Carter lived in a nondescript complex south of downtown in what she thought of as a typical bachelor apartment. A place that was not so much decorated as inhabited. She had the impression that if he had to move suddenly, Carter could be packed within the hour. How much of that came from his transient childhood and how much from the single man's feeling of not wanting to settle down in one place?

"Would you like a drink?" he asked.

"Sure. That would be nice." She set her purse on the table by the sofa and looked around the living room while he went to fix their drinks. Stacks of books teetered at either end of the sofa and on the coffee table. Several framed black-and-white art photos relieved the expanse of white wall behind the sofa, while snapshots crowded a bulletin board near the front door.

"Is rum and cola all right?" he called from the kitchen.

"That's fine. Who are the people in all these pictures?" she asked, walking over for a closer look.

He returned with their drinks. "They're some of the street kids I've stayed in touch with."

She studied the people in the pictures. Most of

them were very young, looking somehow vulnerable despite spiked or dyed hair, tattoos and piercings. Some of them stared at the camera lens, defiant, while other smiled shyly. She recognized Tessa, though the blonde was much thinner in the photograph, and she looked much sadder.

"There are so many," she said, accepting the glass he offered.

"I've been doing this ten years. Seems like there are more every year. A lot of them I can't help."

The regret in his voice brought a lump to her throat. She thought she should say something, something to encourage or comfort him, but he'd already turned away. He walked over to his stereo and began flipping through a stack of CDs. "This is the only tango music I have." He slipped the disk into the stereo. The insistent strains of a saxophone filled the air.

"Who is it?" Joni asked.

"Miguel de Caro. One of the guys at the PD moonlights as a DJ at a Latin club downtown and he turned me on to this." He faced her and held out his hands. "Shall we?"

She set aside her drink and moved into his arms, watching his face as they began to dance. His eyes were focused somewhere over her shoulder, his expression passive, as if he was lost in thought. What was he thinking about? Those children he hadn't been able to help? Or this woman in his arms who refused to let him too close?

Once upon a time, she had thought men were easy to understand. Their needs and emotions seemed so much simpler to figure out than women's. Carter was proving that theory wrong. There were so many facets to him, from tough cop to teen mentor, from elegant dancer to street fighter, from no-nonsense negotiator to determined dreamer. Some parts of him would be so easy to fall in love with, while other aspects made her want to run away.

The music faded and they stopped dancing, though they still held hands, caught in the moment, neither wanting to be the first to break away. A new song began with the seductive calling of a jazz trumpet, followed by soaring strings. Carter pulled her close, guiding her into the steps of the tango once more.

This time they danced more slowly, their movements languid, their bodies liquid as they swayed to the intoxicating music. A single lamp on the table by the sofa cast a golden glow on one corner of the room, throwing the rest of the apartment in shadow. They danced in and out of that circle of light, moving in a sensual rhythm. Carter's hand slid from the small of her back to the curve of her waist, his fingers spanning her hip as he pressed his chest to hers, bending her back across his knee.

She closed her eyes and gave herself up to his embrace, savoring the brush of his shirtfront across her sensitive nipples, the hard muscles of his thigh against her bottom, the taut aching in her groin as she arched toward him. She stumbled a little as he pulled her upright, and he reached out both hands to catch her, wrapping his arms around her and pressing the length of their bodies together.

She writhed against him shamelessly, transformed from passive partner to temptress. She straddled his thigh and shimmied down its length, her eyes locked to his, lips parted in silent invitation.

The heat of his gaze raked over her, and his hands slid up her rib cage, brushing lightly over her breasts before coming to rest on her shoulders. She held back a sigh, craving more than that brief touch.

With swift grace, he pushed her away from him, twirling her until her back was to him, then he brought her crashing against him once more. She could feel his erection, hard against her bottom, and she pressed against him, swiveling her hips, smiling at the low groan that reached her ears.

Hands at her waist, he thrust his knee between her legs, forcing them apart, until she was straddling him again, the fabric of his pants rubbing against her aching arousal, the wet satin of her panties abrading her sensitive center, until she was panting, her vision blurred.

He slid his hands up once more to cup her breasts, the rhythm of the music driving the rhythm of her movements against him. He raked his thumbnails across the points of her breasts through her thin shirt and bra and she moaned. She was aching, on edge, but the contact wasn't enough.

He buried his face in her neck. "Do you want me?" he growled.

"Yes," she gasped.

"Yes, what?"

"Yes, I want you."

"What do you want me to do?" He lightly pinched her nipples and she clenched her thighs around him.

"I...I want you to make love to me," she whispered.

He lifted his hands, holding them away from her, close enough that she could still feel their heat. "Tell me what to do," he whispered.

She tried to turn her head to look at him, but he was holding her too tight against his chest. She licked her lips and tried to think. Sex wasn't something she'd ever talked about before. How could she put into words what she needed from him?

"I...I want you to touch me," she said.

"Where?" His breath tickled the back of her neck, sending a hot shiver down her spine.

"Touch my breasts." She wrapped her fingers around his wrists and dragged his hands up to cover her breasts.

"Touch them with my hands like this?" He caressed her lightly with his fingertips.

She arched against him, pressing into his palms. "Harder."

"Like this?" He massaged her gently, then with more force, rolling the nipples between his fingers.

"Yessss." Head thrust back, eyes closed, she wasn't

sure how much longer she could remain upright while his hands drove her crazy.

"What if I touch you with my mouth? Like this?" He leaned around and began to suckle.

She clamped her thighs around him, straining toward the release she couldn't find. He helped her turn to face him once more. While he continued to caress her breasts with his mouth and tongue, his hands moved up her thighs, stroking, squeezing, inching up to the scant barrier of her panties. He lifted his head and kissed her on the mouth, then on the ear. "Would you like me to touch you...here?" On the last word, he slid two fingers under the elastic of her underwear and into her slick heat.

She bucked against him and groaned, speech lost in this firestorm of feeling. He began to move slowly, in and out. She rocked against his hand, wanting to beg him not to stop, unable to speak.

When his hands did leave her, she opened her eyes and cried out in dismay, but he slid his arms under her back and thighs and lifted her, carrying her through the living room and into the bedroom beyond.

In the light from a streetlamp that shone through the window, she had a dim impression of dark wood furniture and a white comforter draped across a king-size bed. A ceiling fan whirred overhead. Carter laid her down gently and stared into her eyes. "Now what?" he asked.

"Wh-what do you mean?"

"You're calling the shots, remember? You have to tell me what you want."

She took a shaky breath, trying to pull her thoughts into some kind of formation that made sense. She felt taut and edgy, impatient for something she couldn't describe. She stared at the man before her, waiting to do her bidding, and her arousal ratcheted up another notch. She wet her lips and gave him a shaky smile. "Take off your clothes," she said.

He smiled and stepped back, reaching for the top button of his shirt as he did so. With agonizing slowness, he unfastened the buttons, one by one, his eyes never leaving hers.

The shirtfront parted, and he unfastened the cuffs. The streetlamp burnished his chest and shoulders, gilding each muscle. He kicked off his shoes and reached for his belt.

Joni dug her fingers into the comforter, trying to keep still. He unfastened the top button of his pants and drew down the zipper. "Faster," she gasped.

He grinned. "You don't want to wait any longer, do you?" he asked.

"Please. Hurry."

He grasped the waistband of his pants and shoved them to his ankles, along with his briefs. He stripped it all off, along with his socks, then stood before her, naked. "Now what should I do?"

"Undress me. Quickly."

She had to roll to her side so he could reach the zipper, but after that, he had the dress off of her in record time. The breeze from the ceiling fan raised goose bumps on her feverish skin. She reached for him, no longer hesitating to tell him what she needed. "I want you in me. Now."

He took a condom from the bedside table drawer and unwrapped it. She lay on her back and waited for him while he sheathed himself. Then he surprised her once more by rolling her over and lifting her until she straddled him. "You're in charge, remember?" he said with a grin.

She couldn't help but smile in return, but the smile transformed to a gasp as she slid over him. She was so ready for him, so needy. When he began to move beneath her, she closed her eyes and joined him in that urgent rhythm. His hand grasped her hip, guiding her, and she braced against his chest, finding leverage to drive herself more fully onto him.

She arched her head back and caressed her breasts, trying to ease the aching, aching that surged through her, then transformed into pure pleasure. Her climax thundered through her, her muscles trembling with the onslaught. He followed her, his cry of release echoing in the stillness that followed.

She sank down, her head on his chest. His hand came up to rest heavily on her shoulders, like a mantle protecting her. She nestled more snugly against him, and listened as his heartbeat slowed to a steady *thump, thump, thump* beneath her ears. She couldn't remember when she'd ever felt more alive. More at peace. More at home.

9

CARTER WAS NOT a man who sang in the shower, or even along with the radio, but the next morning he found himself humming to himself as he cooked bacon and eggs. *This is what love will do to a man*, he thought as he popped bread into the toaster. *It's embarrassing, and I don't even care.*

To his way of thinking, last night had been a real turning point in his relationship with Joni. They'd really connected, and not just on a physical level. He'd never before been so in tune with another person.

He'd almost told her he loved her last night, but had held back. He didn't want to rush her. But soon, she'd be telling him. He'd seen the love in her eyes last night. Felt it in her body. So maybe he was a romantic fool. But fate had given him this chance at happiness and he was going to make the most of it.

"What time is it?" Joni shuffled into the room, squinting against the bright light. Her hair was tousled and she wore one of his dress shirts, buttoned crookedly. Carter thought she'd never looked sexier.

"It's seven o''clock," he said. "Do you want some coffee?"

She nodded and slumped into a chair at the kitchen

table. He set the cup before her and bent to kiss her cheek. "You look gorgeous. If I didn't have to be at work in half an hour..."

She sipped the coffee and opened her eyes a little wider to take in his uniform shirt and pants. "You have to go to work?"

He turned back to the stove. "I've been trying to figure out a way to get them to pay me to stay home and make love to you, but I'm just not getting through to them." He set a plate of bacon, eggs and toast in front of her. "Do you want jam?"

She nodded, still looking dazed. Shoving her hair off her forehead, she reached for the coffee again. "I didn't think about you having to go to work this morning."

"You know cops work strange schedules—like nurses. My next day off is Wednesday." He refilled his own cup and sat across from her. "Usually I'm off on Tuesday, but I signed on to work a shift for John Curtis."

Coffee sloshed from her cup onto the table and she hurried to mop it up with a paper napkin. "The officer who was shot?"

"Yeah. He's going to be in rehab for five weeks. Hey, what's wrong?" She'd gone white as flour.

"I was working the day they brought him in." She swallowed. "He wasn't wearing a Kevlar vest."

Carter made a face. "Yeah, that was stupid."

She stared at him intently. "Promise me you'll always wear your vest."

He nodded. "Sure, I always wear it."

"Do you have it on now?"

"I usually cook breakfast without it." When she didn't smile, he shifted in his chair. "I'll put it on when I get to the station."

"Put it on now." She gripped her coffee cup, white-knuckled.

"I don't have it here. It's in my locker."

"What good is it going to do you in your locker?" Her eyes filled with tears and her voice shook.

He leaned across the table and put his hand on her shoulder. "Hey, it's okay. Nothing's going to happen to me on the way to the station."

She jerked away from him and shoved back her chair. "You don't know that. Some nut might see your uniform and decide to take out a cop. Or you might decide to play hero again and get in a fight with a thief who has a gun." She got up and slammed her dishes into the sink.

He stared at her back. "What's going on with you this morning?"

She shook her head. "You don't understand, do you?"

"No, I don't. Because you're not making any sense." He stood, but didn't move toward her.

She turned to face him, her back against the sink. "You work at a job that's dangerous, but you don't see anything wrong with taking stupid risks. You probably get off on risk." She shook her head. "Of course you do. You wouldn't be a cop if you didn't."

"That's as stupid as my saying you became a nurse because you like the idea of catching diseases from your patients. Or my thinking you were going to get AIDS because you work in an emergency room."

"It's not the same."

"It's exactly the same." He slammed down his cup and crossed his arms over his chest. "Tell me, why wouldn't you get AIDS working in a place where you come into contact with blood on a regular basis?"

"We take precautions, wear gloves and masks, screen patients—"

"And cops take precautions, too. I don't go out there every day thinking, 'Today I'm going to lay my life on the line." No, I'm thinking, 'How can I stay out of trouble and save my hide?' I want to come home alive every day."

I want to come home to you. But he didn't say it. Couldn't say it. Not when she was looking at him as if she hated him.

He glanced at the clock. "Damn. I have to go," he said. He fished his keys from his pocket and tossed them to her. "Take my truck. I'll catch the bus. We'll talk more later, when you've had time to calm down."

"When I've had time to calm down? I am perfectly calm!"

But he was already gone, slamming the door behind him.

It was probably a bad idea to run out on an argument with a woman, but better that than say something he'd later regret. He checked his watch again. He had time to catch the 7:26 bus.

He'd just reached the bus stop when a car drove by, sending a shower of water over him. He scowled down at his wet shoes and pants. It figured. Half an hour ago, he'd been on top of the world. A few minutes later, he'd ridden a rocket ship to the bottom.

JONI WAS SCARED. Terrified of the feelings surging through her. For a while last night she'd thought if she loved Carter enough, his job wouldn't matter anymore. But then she'd seen him this morning in his uniform, and his mention of Officer Curtis had filled her head with pictures of a different man in that same uniform, lying on a stretcher, bleeding and in pain. It was like a sudden vision of the future, what was in store for her if she was crazy enough to get involved with a man who thought risking his life was a good way to make a living.

All she wanted to do now was get away. Away from Carter and the way he made her feel. The way he made her *think*.

She raced around his bedroom, gathering up her clothes, coming to a standstill when she found her panties, ripped at both sides. The memory of Carter's fingers caressing her robbed the strength from her knees, and she sank onto the bed, fighting back sobs. No man had ever made her feel the way Carter did. What if she never had a chance to feel that way again?

Somehow, she mustered the strength to finish

dressing, leaving her panties crumpled on the rug. The erotic sensation of being naked beneath her dress unnerved her, but she forced herself not to think about it as she shoved her feet into her shoes and headed for the door. Locking it from the inside, she went downstairs to wait for her cab. She'd combed her hair and washed her face, but she knew she looked a wreck. What did it matter? She felt even worse than she looked.

Ignoring the cab driver's smirk as he took in her rumpled dress and bare face, she gave him her address and settled back in the seat. She was going to go home, take a shower, put on her pajamas and crawl into bed. She didn't want to see anybody, talk to anyone, or think about anything. Not until the pain was bearable—say, in another year or two.

When she entered her apartment, her answering machine flashed that she had three messages, but she ignored it on her way to the bathroom. She didn't have anything to say to anyone right now. Especially not Carter.

She was drying her hair when the phone started ringing. She let the machine pick up, and felt a stab of guilt as G.P.'s voice came on the speaker. "Joni, I want to hear how the dance lesson went," she said. "Did you have a wonderful time?"

She stared at the phone, guilt tying a knot in her stomach. G.P. was going to have to know the truth sooner or later. Joni might as well get it over with.

She snatched up the receiver. "Hi, G.P."

"Hello, darling. How was the dance lesson?"

"It was great." That part was true. She'd never believed she could have such a good time dancing.

"I knew you'd love it! Tell me everything. What did you learn?"

"We learned the tango. Well, I learned. Carter already knew how." *He'd* been the reason her evening was so enjoyable. He'd made every minute of the lesson fun. She shut her eyes against the painful memories.

"A man who can dance is a rare gem these days," G.P. said. "You picked a good one."

She swallowed. "About Carter, G.P.—"

"I know, you think I'm rushing you. But I hate to see you two wasting any more time when it's obvious you're so in love."

Joni twisted the end of the bath towel into a knot. "We're not in love, G.P. It...it was just an act."

The silence on the other end of the line made her wonder if the phone had gone dead. "What are you talking about?" G.P. finally asked.

She sat on the end of the bed, too weary to stand any longer. "Carter and I were just pretending. To fool you." She felt as if she'd swallowed an anchor. Why had she ever thought lying to her grandmother would be a good thing?

"But why would you want to fool me?"

"I wanted you to think I already had a boyfriend so you wouldn't think you had to find one for me. I...I wanted to make my own choice, but I knew you wouldn't take no for an answer."

The answering silence made her feel small. She swallowed tears. "G.P...I'm sorry. I didn't mean to hurt you."

"No, I'm the one who should apologize. But what you saw as meddling was only my attempt to see you happy. I want you to find someone who can make you as happy as I was with your grandfather."

"I will find someone someday but...but Carter's not the one." She choked back a sob as tears spilled down her face.

G.P. waited for her to regain control before she spoke again. "Listen to yourself! You're crying buckets over a man you say you care nothing about?"

Joni sniffed and wiped her eyes on the edge of the towel. "Carter is...a friend. But he's not the right man for me."

"I think he is."

"But G.P.—"

"No, you *listen* to me. I may be old, but I'm no fool. And I know what I saw when you two were together. You love that man and he loves you. No Academy Award-winning actor could have faked those feelings."

Joni shook her head. "You're wrong, G.P. It was all an act."

"You can lie to me, child, and I'll forgive you. But it's an even bigger sin to lie to yourself." There was a click, and the dial tone buzzed in Joni's ear.

She stared at the receiver. G.P. had hung up on her!

The sobs came in earnest now. She replaced the phone in the cradle and crawled under the covers. Her life was a disaster. She'd let herself fall for the wrong man, and now her grandmother was mad at her. Joni couldn't blame her. She was angry with herself for ending up in this mess.

She pulled the covers over her head and squeezed her eyes shut. She wanted to sleep and wake up to find this had all been a dream. Tomorrow she'd get up and go to work and have her normal, boring life back. It had been lonely at times and not particularly exciting, but at least it hadn't demanded such intense emotions. From ecstasy to agony in one day was a ride she didn't care to go on again.

Joni woke to the annoying trill of the doorbell. She shoved the covers off her head and sat up, disoriented. Light shone under the blinds and a glance at the clock told her it was 6:00 p.m. She'd slept all afternoon.

The bell rang again. Grabbing her robe, she stumbled to the door. "I'm coming."

She stood on tiptoe to look out the peephole, and found Carter staring up at her. He was frowning. "Let me in," he demanded.

She clutched her robe more tightly around herself, aware that she was naked beneath the thin layer of silk. "I don't have your truck," she called through the door. "I took a cab home."

"This isn't about my truck. We have to talk."

She didn't want to talk to him. Talking to him was too hard right now and seeing him was worse, but she knew he'd stay out in the hallway, ringing her bell, until she let him in. Reluctantly, she unfastened the chain and opened the door.

He strode into the room, his handsome features transformed by a forbidding scowl. He was still in his uniform, the shirt stretched tight across his shoulders, radiating strength. He paced across the carpet, fists clenched at his sides. "Do you want to tell me what the hell is going on?"

She moved back, putting as much distance as possible between them, and struggled to keep her voice calm. "It's over."

He stopped pacing and stared at her. "What's over?"

"This whole charade." She took a deep breath. "I told G.P. the truth—that you and I have been pretending in order to fool her."

In three steps, he closed the distance between them. She shrank back, but he made no move to touch her. "So that's what all this has been for you? Last night when you were begging me to make love to you, you were just pretending?"

She forced herself to look at him, though she couldn't bring herself to meet his eyes. Instead, she focused on his mouth, drawn down now in a frown. "I was pretending we could have a future together. This morning, I realized none of it was true."

"Because I'm a cop."

She nodded. "I'm sorry, but I...I don't have it in me to risk that much. Better to break it off now before we get too serious."

The muscles of his jaw knotted as he clamped his mouth shut. She glanced up and his gaze caught and held her. His eyes said everything words couldn't, telegraphing hurt and anger, and underneath it all, raw desire for all that had been denied him. His gaze stripped her naked, revealing all her secrets. She hugged her arms across her chest. "I...I'm sorry it worked out this way."

He took a step back, putting some distance between them, collecting himself. When he spoke, his voice was calm. "You're forgetting one thing."

"Wh-what's that?"

"You still owe me."

She blinked, confused. "Owe you what?"

"Our agreement was that after my stint as pretend boyfriend ended, you'd go on one date with me."

"Oh that." She looked away. How could she endure a whole evening alone with Carter when even standing here now had her on the verge of breaking down? "I really don't think—"

"Uh-uh. I won't let you off the hook on this one. We had a deal. One date."

She hugged herself more tightly and squeezed her eyes shut. He wasn't going to back down. And why should he? She'd made a promise. She was obligated to keep it. "All right. One date." She could handle that, couldn't she? It wouldn't be easy, but she'd do it, if only to prove to him that she meant what she said. She wouldn't become involved with a man who could hurt her so much.

He took a step back toward the door. "Next Friday night then. I'll pick you up at seven."

"All right."

"I guess I'll call the studio and cancel our next dance lesson."

Her stomach twisted, remembering how wonderful and yes, romantic, their last lesson had been. She nodded, unable to speak.

He opened the door, then paused again, his hand on the knob. His gaze swept over her again, searing her. "Wear something nice. I've got big plans for us."

10

JONI FULLY EXPECTED G.P. to spend that week trying to change her mind. She wouldn't have been surprised if Carter hadn't shown up a time or two also to remind her of what she was missing. Instead, both her grandmother and Carter were conspicuously absent from her life, leaving her with no one to blame for her current state of misery but herself.

By the time she arrived home from work on Friday, she was worn out from sleepless nights and angst-ridden days. She'd broken up with men before, but it had never been a physically painful experience, one that left her aching and irritable.

If this was what it was like to be in love, why did anyone go through it? She alternated between being anxious to see Carter again and dreading the moment. What would she say to him? What would she do? How could she keep from blurting out how much she still wanted him? Their date was tonight and she still didn't know how she should act.

She sorted through the mail, stopping at the sight of familiar handwriting on a square white envelope. The card inside bore a picture of a shiny red heart. Inside G.P. had written: *I know you don't want any more advice from me, but as your grandmother it's my duty to give it to you anyway. You don't want to get to be my age and look back with regret on all the things you didn't do. So be careful in the choices you make. If in doubt, I find it's always best to follow your heart. Love, G.P.*

For G.P., the simple message showed remarkable restraint, and maybe a little of how much she felt Joni's hurt. *Follow your heart*, she said. If only it were that simple. Joni's heart told her she loved Carter. He was like no man she'd ever met before. At times over the past week, she'd seriously wondered if she'd be able to live without him.

If she followed her heart, she wouldn't hesitate to declare her love for him, come what may. But that other ruling organ, her brain, kept getting in the way. G.P., of all people, ought to understand her reluctance to get involved with Carter. G.P. had lost the person who was dearest to her in the world when her husband was killed in an airplane crash, and she'd suffered greatly with the pain of that loss. Wasn't it better to get out of a situation with that kind of potential as soon as possible, before too much damage had been done? If it hurt now for Joni to give up Carter, wouldn't it hurt that much more two or ten or twenty years from now?

She checked the clock. She'd better get moving if she was going to be ready by seven for her date. Date. The word made her heart flutter. She tried to tell herself this wasn't a real romantic date. This was an obligation. Part of the deal she'd made with Carter.

Liar. The accusation echoed in her head as she stood under the shower. She was looking forward to seeing Carter. She'd been missing him all week. That made it all the more difficult to know how to handle seeing him tonight.

As she dried her hair, she thought about the message in the card G.P. had sent her: *You don't want to get to be my age and look back with regret on all the things you didn't do.*

Was she going to regret sending Carter away after tonight? She closed her eyes and took a deep breath. Truth time. No more lies. If she sent Carter away, she would regret it. G.P. was right—Joni did love Carter, and he'd made it clear he loved her. So why couldn't they work things out?

Work. She laid down her hairbrush, shaken by a sudden thought. Why hadn't she thought of this before? The obstacle here wasn't Carter. The problem was his job. If he changed that, there would be no reason for them not to be together.

Her heart raced at the thought. What if Carter stopped being a police officer? He'd said himself he wasn't defined by his job. There must be all kinds of things he could do instead. He could be some kind of counselor, working with teens. He'd enjoy that kind of work, and he'd be good at it.

He said he loved her. He was a romantic man who believed in fate. Maybe fate had sent her into his life to get him out of his dangerous job. Once she talked to him about it, she was sure he'd see that.

Suddenly, the feeling of dread she'd carried around all week left her. She danced around the room, humming a tango melody. Tonight was going to be wonderful. Life-changing. She and Carter *could* be happy together. She couldn't wait to tell him.

She tossed aside the black pants and sweater she'd picked out and instead pulled out the little red dress she'd bought for their "honeymoon." Carter's eyes had popped when he'd seen this dress before and she wanted the same reaction from him tonight as they celebrated this new direction in their relationship. Things were going to be better than ever for them from now on.

She took extra care with her hair and makeup. By the time she checked the clock again, it was ten to seven. Carter would be here any minute now....

By seven-fifteen, she was beginning to worry. Carter had never been late before.

By seven-thirty, she was pacing.

At eight o'clock, she called his apartment. No answer. He was probably on his way. Maybe stuck in traffic.

At eight-fifteen, she found his cell-phone number and called it. After three rings, a recorded voice informed her, "The person you are trying to reach is unavailable at this time."

At eight twenty-five, she opened a bottle of wine and poured herself a glass. All sorts of thoughts ran through her head. Was Carter hurt somewhere? Or worse, was he deliberately trying to hurt her? It didn't seem like him, but he'd been so angry with her the last time she'd seen him. Maybe standing her up was his way of paying her back.

At nine o'clock, she put the bottle of wine back in the refrigerator and took off the red dress. As she cleaned off her makeup, the tears started and refused to stop. She lay across the bed and cried until, worn out from worry and hurt, she fell into a fitful sleep.

JUNE BUGS DARTED around the light over Joni's front door as Carter climbed the steps to her apartment. He knew he had no business showing up here at this hour, but he couldn't stay away. He checked his watch. One o'clock. Six hours past the time he was supposed to have picked her up. He'd be lucky if she didn't hit him over the head with a vase or something.

It didn't matter. He couldn't stand to be alone right now.

He leaned against the doorbell. *Please, Joni. Let me in.*

He was about to hit the doorbell a second time when he heard the lock turn. He straightened, bracing himself for the chewing-out he probably deserved. But Joni took one look at him and her expression softened. She took his arm and tugged him into the apartment. "Carter, what happened?" she asked. "You look awful."

"I'm sorry I stood you up," he said. "I know I should have called, but..." He shrugged. He should have done a lot of things, but he couldn't go back and fix that now.

"Sit down over here." She led him to the sofa. "Do you want coffee?"

"Coffee would be great." He sank onto the sofa and leaned his head back against the cushion, shutting his eyes. Big mistake. The events of the night replayed themselves across his eyelids in Technicolor horror. He snapped his eyes open again and straightened, turning to watch Joni. He had come here because he knew she could distract him, help him forget what he'd seen.

He wondered how long she'd waited up for him, how long she'd sat by the door, all dressed up, before she changed into the pajamas she now wore. Her face had the slightly puffy look of someone who'd been crying.

He swallowed against the tightness in his own throat. What kind of a man was he, to leave a woman crying like that?

She returned and sat beside him. "The coffee's brewing." She took his hand. "Your hands are ice-cold! What happened?"

He didn't want to talk about it. Didn't want to think about it. But he owed Joni an explanation. He wiped his hand over his face, beard stubble rasping against his palm. Where to begin?

"I got a call this afternoon from one of the street kids. A girl named Luz. She's maybe sixteen, ran away from home when she was fourteen. She's smart and I've been working on her, trying to get her to a shelter, where she could live and go to school." He shook his head. "She says she's not ready yet. Anyway, she called me tonight to tell me this guy she's friends with, Tino, was in trouble, and she asked if I would come talk to him. So I said sure, I'd come over there and talk to him for a little bit, see what I could do."

He leaned forward, elbows on his knees, and looked out over the darkened living room. A pair of red high heels rested on their sides in front of the couch, where Joni had probably kicked them off while she was waiting for him tonight. He glanced at her. "I should have called, but I didn't think I'd be gone that long."

She patted his hand. "It's okay. Tell me about Tino."

"Tino." He took a deep breath. "Tall, skinny kid. Hell, they're all skinny. Too many drugs and not enough food. Maybe fifteen. He hasn't been around here very long I don't think. Luz had me meet her down on Commerce and we drove to this abandoned factory a few blocks away where some of the kids crash. It's not much of a place, but it gets them out of the weather. They've dragged some old mattresses and a beat-up sofa inside, and Tino was there."

He stopped talking, seeing the scene again in his mind: sunlight streaming through the broken windows high in the walls, Tino stretched out on the sofa, five or six other kids standing a little ways away, watching, their eyes wide with fear. The smell of piss and unwashed bodies stole his breath away, but the anguished look on those kids' faces made him move forward.

"What was wrong with Tino?" Joni prompted, her voice soft, as reassuring as her presence beside him.

"I thought at first maybe he was on a bad trip." He glanced at her. "Street drugs come laced with all kinds of stuff. Sometimes kids get ahold of something mixed with poison, or even something too pure for them to handle." He shook his head. "That wasn't it this time, though.

"When I got close to him, I could see his eyes were open. Luz told him I was her friend, Carter. No mention that I was a cop, though I already knew the others in the room, so Tino probably knew who I was and what I did for a living. 'What's going on?' I asked him.

"He didn't look at me, just kept staring at the ceiling. 'I'm dead,' he said.

"'You look alive to me.'

"He shook his head. 'I'm as good as dead.'"

Luz had started crying then, making whimpering noises and wiping her eyes on the tail of her shirt. One of the other girls came over and put her arm around Luz. "He stole an 8 Ball from the Varrio Kings," *the other girl, Caro, said.* "They've put a hit on him."

"I don't understand," Joni's voice pulled him back to the present. "Why would he say something like that?"

Carter rubbed the back of his neck. Fatigue was fast catching up to him. "As far as I can tell, Tino swiped some cocaine from a gang member. The gang—the Varrio Kings, or VKs—found out and let it be known they intended to kill him."

"But you could protect him, couldn't you?"

The simple faith in her words made his gut twist. If only things were that easy. "I told him if he'd come with me, I'd find a safe place for him. He said there wasn't any safe place, but that that was okay, he was ready to die."

Joni gasped. "He's only fifteen!"

Carter nodded. "These kids have seen a lot in those years. Some of them have suffered a lot. I guess he figured he didn't have anything to live for."

"What did you do?"

"I sent the other kids away and I sat and talked with him for a while." He'd spent two hours sitting on the dirty concrete floor beside the couch, much of it in silence. Tino alternated between frantic bursts of speech and long minutes when he refused to even acknowledge Carter's presence. The boy's long black hair fell across his forehead, obscuring his eyes, and the beginnings of a mustache blended with the dirt on his face. He wore a too-large T-shirt with the sleeves ripped out and had a homemade tattoo of a lightning bolt on the arm closest to Carter.

"I wanted to call you, but my cell phone didn't have a signal inside the building, and I was afraid to leave him for even a second."

"Do you think the gang was looking for him?"

"I think they probably knew where he was and were waiting for him to come out."

"Why didn't you call for someone to come help you take him away?"

"He hadn't committed a crime that I could prove, except maybe trespassing. I couldn't call a unit for that. If he went with me, he had to do it under his own power."

"Did you finally convince him?"

"I thought so. Some time in the third hour, he said if I would shut up, he'd come with me." He hung his head. "I was so relieved, I did something really stupid."

"What was that?"

"He said he wanted to grab his things from the next room. I should have gone with him, but just then Caro and Luz came back and I stayed to talk with them. Five minutes later, I realized Tino was taking too long. I ran into the other room and saw the door standing open."

"He ran away?"

Carter nodded. "I ran after him, figuring he couldn't have gone far. When I didn't find him right away, I got in the car and started driving. I even got on the radio and asked patrol to keep an eye out for him and to let me know if they spotted him."

She moved closer and laced her fingers in his. "Did you find him?"

"Not for a long time. I cruised the area for hours.

Luz told me Tino didn't have any money, so I figured he couldn't have gone too far on foot. I was about ready to give up when one of the patrol officers radioed that he'd spotted a boy that fit Tino's description running down San Augustine. I drove over there and parked, then set out on foot."

The streets had been full of people, a Friday night crowd out having fun. Bars and restaurants spilled people and music onto the sidewalks. Passing cars added the sweep of headlights and the honk of horns to the confusion of sights and sounds. Carter pushed his way through the press of people, ignoring their shouts and laughter as he searched for a tall, skinny boy with long black hair.

He spotted him about a block ahead and broke into a run, prepared to tackle him if he had to. He collided with a beefy tourist, who complained loudly in a Brooklyn twang. Tino looked back, saw Carter, and took off running.

"I spotted him but then lost him after half a block, but I kept looking for him, checking doorways and alleys. I was sure Tino was close. Then gunfire exploded nearby. Women screamed and people began running, panicked. I heard tires squeal as a car took off down the street.

"I found Tino in an alley. He'd been shot."

The boy had been slumped against the wall in the fetid darkness. A pocket flashlight revealed a gunshot wound to the chest. He opened his eyes as Carter knelt beside him. "I told you I was a dead man," he whispered, *then slumped into Carter's arms.*

"I waited with him until the ambulance arrived, but I knew it was too late." He'd felt the life slip away as he held the boy in his arms.

Afterward, he'd had to go to the station to file a report. Then he'd showered and changed clothes.

Now he reached for Joni's hand. "I know it's late, but I couldn't stand to go home alone."

"No. I'm glad you came here." She patted his hand. "I'll get the coffee."

She returned with two cups. The aroma of the coffee mingled with the vanilla of her perfume. He inhaled deeply, his fatigue receding. "You did everything you could," she said, handing him a cup and sitting beside him again.

"Everything except save his life."

"You shouldn't blame yourself."

"But I do." Who else was there to blame, except whatever faceless beings were responsible for a world full of Tinos and Luzes and Caros?

They sipped their coffee, neither of them speaking. Carter felt talked out. He closed his eyes, listening to the sounds of everyday life: the clink of a coffee mug against the glass top of the coffee table, the tick of the clock, the rustle of silk as Joni moved. He breathed deeply, trying to battle back the blackness that threatened to engulf him.

"What can I do to help you?" she asked.

He opened his eyes to find her watching him, her

eyes filled with concern. He set his coffee cup aside and looked into her eyes, hoping he could make her understand what he had no words for. "I need to forget about death for a while," he said.

She nodded and reached for him, her arms encircling him, drawing him into her embrace. "Think about life," she whispered. "About how wonderful it feels to be alive."

She kissed him gently, her lips barely brushing his. He pulled her closer, deepening the kiss, pressing her body against his. The feel of her, so warm and alive, made the horror of the last few hours recede.

She broke off the kiss and smiled at him, then took his hand and tugged him toward the bedroom. The bed was a silk-covered island bathed in the light of the bedside lamps. They stopped beside it and he pulled her to him once more.

While they kissed, she slid her hands between them and unfastened the buttons of his shirt. Then she undid his belt, and the top button of his pants. She stroked her fingers over his fly, tracing the outline of his erection, and he felt himself leap at her touch.

She pulled back far enough to look into his eyes, and then she pushed the shirt back over his shoulders. Next, she helped him out of the rest of his clothes, until he stood before her, naked.

He reached for her again, but she urged him gently toward the bed. "Lie down and watch."

He crawled onto the bed, then rolled onto his side

to watch her as she undressed. She removed her clothes slowly, smiling as she studied his face. She released the buttons of her top one by one, revealing first the shadow of her cleavage, then the inner curve of her breasts, and then the entire breasts themselves, full and round. When she slid the top off her shoulders, the movement thrust her breasts forward. They swayed softly, the peaks tight with arousal. Carter ached to touch her, but forced himself to lie still and continue watching.

She turned her back to him before she lowered her pants, sliding the elastic waistband down oh-so-slowly, gradually revealing her softly rounded bottom. Carter's mouth went dry and he had to remind himself to breathe.

When she faced him again, she was naked, the curves and planes of her body burnished and shadowed by the soft light. "You're gorgeous," he said.

Still smiling, she lay beside him and kissed him again, sliding her hands down the length of his body in long, soothing strokes. He kissed her mouth, her eyes, her ears, then rested his face against the vanilla-scented softness of her throat. He gathered her breasts in his hands, filling up the emptiness inside himself with the sight and scent and feel of her. Life ebbed back into him with each caress. "It feels so good just to touch you," he said.

"I want you to touch me. And I want you to let me touch you." She put her hands on his shoulders and urged him onto his back. Moving down, she traced her tongue around his nipples, lavishing attention on first one, then the other, before laying a trail of kisses to his navel. She scooted down farther, kissing and caressing his thighs. He watched, mesmerized by the pleasure she took in exploring him this way. She smiled up at him, then playfully licked his shaft, the one flick of her tongue making him jerk in response. "So you liked that?" she asked.

"Oh yeah."

"Then what about this?" She took him into the velvet softness of her mouth. He closed his eyes and moaned, losing himself in the wave of sensation.

He opened his eyes again when she left him, and started to protest, but she returned quickly and deftly unrolled a condom. She sheathed him, her hands caressing him, then straddled him, bracing her hands on his chest and smiling as she slid over him, embracing him in her liquid heat.

He let out a low groan and smoothed his hand along her thighs, then up her sides to cup her breasts. She began to move, almost leaving him before driving down once more, each stroke more powerful than the one before, building the tension within him until his breath came in gasps and his heart beat like a war drum. He grasped her hips, trying to tell her to move more slowly, that he would wait for her to catch up with him. But she only smiled and reached one hand around to trail her fingernails across his balls, sending him hurtling over the edge. He groaned and drove into her with the force of his climax, all pain wiped away in that incredible release.

When they finally lay still again, she slid off of him and lay beside him, her body pressed to his, head resting on his chest. He felt spent. Sated. And incredibly lucky.

He kissed her shoulder. "Thank you," he whispered.

She nuzzled closer. "Thank you for what?"

"For understanding. For knowing just what I needed."

She put her finger to his lips. "Shhhh. We'll talk tomorrow. Now you need to sleep."

An hour ago, he would have said he might never sleep peacefully again. Now he knew he would, as long as he was in her arms.

11

THE NEXT MORNING, Joni was awakened by an unfamiliar weight across her body. As consciousness returned, she realized it was Carter's arm and leg draped across her, hugging her close to him. She shut her eyes and snuggled closer, relishing this feeling of being so cherished that even in sleep, he didn't want to be apart from her. Would waking up next to him every morning be this nice?

He stirred and mumbled something unintelligible. He buried his face in the back of her neck and his hand came up to rest on her breast. She squirmed and felt the hard heat of his erection nudge at her bottom. Smiling, she tried to wriggle out of his reach, but he pulled her back. "Oh no you don't. It's time we finished what we started last night."

Laughing, she rolled away from him, but her laughter changed to a gasp when he leaned over and took her breast in his mouth. He circled her nipple with his tongue, while his hand made corresponding circles across her stomach, each circle dipping lower, teasing her with the promise of a more intimate touch. She had not known her body could come awake so suddenly, the memory of last night's arousal returning as if only minutes, instead of hours, had passed.

Carter caressed her thighs, sliding his hand beneath her to squeeze her bottom, before finally coming to rest between her legs. She felt the heat and the weight of him just above her aching sex, and arched toward him, silently pleading with him to touch her more.

Leaving his hand on her, he slid back up and began kissing her neck. The brief, soft brushes of his tongue made every nerve tingle with awareness of him. Even the scrape of his beard against her skin heightened her arousal. He feathered kisses down the side of her breast and across her stomach. "Do you remember when you did this to me last night?" he asked, his voice vibrating against her stomach.

"Yes." In fact, she could barely remember anything in this onslaught of sensation.

"I hope it feels even half as wonderful for you as it did for me." He continued on down her body, at last reaching the center of her arousal. He parted her folds with his tongue and began to stroke and suckle, gently at first, then with more force, until she was arched against the bed, gripping the rumpled sheets in her fists, panting and moaning, past the edge of control. Her release came quickly, a sunburst of heat and light flooding through her.

When she regained her senses, she realized she was smiling. She opened her eyes to find Carter smiling too as he slid into her and began to move in that intoxicating rhythm she could not fail to follow.

Their coupling this morning had a languid beauty to it, a slow, sensuous dance that might have been set to the music of the tango. She took the time to run her hands across his back, appreciating the strength of muscle and bone, to admire the olive hue of his skin against her milky fairness, to savor the slide of his flesh beneath her hand. She closed her eyes and welcomed the tension building in her once more, this sweet acknowledgment of her desire and love for this man.

She felt the tremor of his climax shudder through her, her body tightening around him in response, building once more toward her own release, which was gentler this time, but no less satisfying.

They lay together afterward, on the verge of dozing, her head on his shoulder, her fingers idly tangling in the coarse dusting of hair on his chest. He covered her hand with his own. "That tickles."

"Oh, you're ticklish, are you?" She feinted toward his belly.

He grabbed that hand also. "Don't you dare."

Laughing, she sat up, letting her hair fall forward, the ends brushing his chest. She loved to see him smiling. Last night, when she'd opened the door, his expression of raw grief and pain had alarmed her. She'd known before he said a word that something horrible had happened. Something she never wanted him to have to go through again. "Want some break-fast?" she asked.

He reached his arms overhead, lengthening his body in a stretch that sent every muscle into relief and made her mouth go dry. "Why don't we take a shower first?" he said.

She shook her head and crawled backward toward the edge of the bed. If she got into the shower with Carter, they might never get dressed today. And they needed to dress, and talk about their future. "You hit the shower. I'll make breakfast."

Fifteen minutes later, when she brought him coffee, he was shaving, his wet hair curling around his face, a towel knotted at his hips. She paused in the door-way to watch as he guided a disposable razor down his cheek. Looking at him this way, so at home in her home, turned her insides to mush. It was a feeling she could learn to like.

"I've been thinking." She set the mug of coffee on the edge of the sink.

He slid his gaze toward her. "Yes?"

"About us."

He wiped the razor on a towel and reached for her hand. "Whatever you're going to say, there's one thing you have to know."

She held her breath. "What is that?"

"I love you." He kissed her cheek, then wiped away a smudge of shaving cream with his thumb. "Just in case I hadn't been clear on that before."

"I...I know you love me." She took a deep breath

and said the words that had been repeating in her head all week. "And I love you, too."

He turned back to the mirror, watching her reflection there, as if he didn't trust himself to look at her directly. "So where does that leave us now?"

"I've had a lot of time this week to think about things. And I think I've come up with a solution to everything else that was bothering me."

"You mean my being a cop?"

"Yes." She straightened, hoping she looked calmer than she felt. "After what happened last night, I'm sure you'll agree that the only thing for you to do is to quit your job."

The razor clattered against the sink as it fell. He turned to stare at her. "What?"

"I think you should quit your job. Nothing says you have to be a cop. There's no reason for you to be out there every day risking your life."

He snatched up a towel and wiped the rest of the shaving cream from his face. "What else do you expect me to do?"

"Anything. You could be a teacher. Or a counselor. You could work for an organization that helps at-risk youth. I'm sure you have all kinds of contacts through the work you've been doing." She frowned at him. She'd expected him to be more excited by her idea. Why couldn't he see all the possibilities for his life?

His voice was tighteningly quiet. "So you think it's that easy? Just chuck everything I've worked for for ten years out the window because you can't handle it?''

"It's not just me. I saw you last night, remember? I know how much this job takes out of you."

"What about what it gives me? Doesn't that count for anything?" He threw off the towel and grabbed up a pair of briefs and pulled them on, then reached for his jeans.

She stared at him. "What are you doing?"

"I'm leaving." He zipped the jeans, then pulled on his shirt and pushed past her, into the bedroom.

She followed him. "You can't walk out now. We have to talk."

"I don't have anything else to say." He sat on the edge of the bed and put on shoes and socks, then headed out of the room, buttoning his shirt as he walked.

She followed him to the front door. "I don't see why you're so upset. Why you won't even consider—"

He whipped around, his hands outstretched as if to grab her, but they fell to his sides before they ever made contact. "What if I asked you to stop being a nurse because I didn't like it?"

She hugged her arms across her chest, ignoring an uncomfortable feeling in her stomach. "That's different. My job isn't dangerous. There's no reason for me to give it up."

"And there's no reason for me to stop being a cop—except that apparently I'm not worth your taking any kind of risk." He jabbed his finger at her. "I've got news for you. Life is all about risk. Accept that and move on."

"You said you loved me."

"And you said you loved me. That has to mean all of me. My job is part of who I am. If you love me, you have to love all of me."

Then he left, slamming the door behind him. She stared at the closed door, feeling sick and stupid. All she'd wanted was to make things right between them, to spare them both the hurt his job could bring him—the kind of hurt he'd suffered last night.

Yes, suggesting that he change careers was asking a lot, but why wouldn't he even consider the possibilities open to him? Why couldn't he see that she was trying to help them both? Did his job mean more to him than his feelings for her? Or was she wrong to expect that much from love?

CARTER GRIPPED the steering wheel, white-knuckled, choking on the knot of anger and hurt that rose in his throat. How could Joni say she loved him one minute and ask him to totally change his life for her the next? Wasn't love all about accepting the other person for what he was?

His job was part of who he was, and if Joni couldn't see that, maybe she wasn't really in love with him, but only with an idea of him—not the man he really was, but the man she wanted him to be.

If she had lashed out at him with a knife, she

couldn't have hurt him more. Did she even realize that? Did she know how much power she had to wound him, precisely because he cared for her?

And he did care for her. Deeply. More than he'd ever cared for anyone else. It wasn't an emotion he could turn on and off with a switch; it was part of him now.

The white heat of his anger faded, leaving behind a dragging fatigue. He steered the truck into the parking lot of his apartment and parked, then laid his head against the steering wheel and closed his eyes. What was he going to do now? He felt like crawling into bed and sleeping for a year, or maybe punching something until the pain from the exertion to his body overwhelmed the pain squeezing his heart.

He sat up again, mustering his strength. Better to fight than to crawl under the covers and hide. Part of what made him a good cop was that he wasn't a quitter.

He climbed out of the truck and pounded up the stairs to his apartment. For the first time, he noticed how uninviting the rooms were, like a hotel room designed for occupants who were only passing through. After a childhood spent moving around, he'd developed the habit of never leaving an imprint on his surroundings. He'd never been one place long enough to feel at home.

He'd thought Joni was the one he'd make a home with at last. But he hadn't thought having that home would require having to give up so much of himself.

He went into the bedroom to change out of the clothes he'd borrowed last night from his locker at the station. He'd thrown out the others, which had been soaked with blood. He shook his head. Poor Tino. How do you make a kid believe in himself enough to want to accept the help that was offered? A lot of them never would believe, but enough of them did that he had to keep trying.

That's what Joni didn't understand—the need in him to keep trying. She wasn't able to see past her fear to the good in all that he did. She didn't want to understand. His job was the deal breaker for her. If he wouldn't leave it, then he would have to leave her.

"Damn her!" He jerked open a drawer and reached for a clean pair of underwear. Why did he have to fall for a woman he couldn't reason with? An infuriating, stubborn, aggravating...

His fingers closed around cool silk, every nerve responding instantly to the sensory memory of feminine flesh sheathed in this luxurious bit of cloth. He held up the scrap of white fabric that had once been Joni's panties before he had torn them from her body and carried her to his bed.

A wave of desire hit him like the aftershock of an explosion, almost knocking him to his knees. All the cursing and ranting in the world wouldn't get her out of her system. No amount of liquor would drown this wanting in him. And no matter how often he told himself he could get along just fine without her, his heart would always know he was lying.

Fate had sent her to him, but if he was going to keep her, he would have to fight. Not with fists or with words, but by taking the thing she'd offered him—her love—and turning it back on her to make her see his world through his eyes. He'd show her that what she saw as danger was a small tradeoff for living a life that made a difference.

If he could find a way to accomplish that, then he just might have a chance.

GRIEF IMMOBILIZED JONI, blurring time and robbing her of the ability to think or act coherently. For two days, she moped around her apartment in her bathrobe. The inside of her eyelids felt like sandpaper from crying, her nose looked like part of a Christmas pageant costume and her stomach ached from a diet of chocolate ice cream and white wine. Everywhere she looked she was reminded of Carter: their uneaten congealed breakfast sat in the kitchen sink, the towels he'd used lay in a heap on the bathroom floor, and the sheets on her bed still carried his scent.

She knew now why people in some cultures covered the mirrors when a loved one died: every time she saw her reflection, she recoiled in horror. Why would any man want to have anything to do with such a pathetic excuse for a woman?

She couldn't even muster the energy to go to work. She'd called in sick and had refused to answer the phone. If it was Carter calling, she didn't trust herself to talk to him.

She still wanted him too much, a fact that ran repeatedly through her mind like a broken CD. She tried to tell herself that time would dim her pain and make it possible for her to think clearly—even dress herself once more—but at the rate things were progressing, she might very well be too old to worry about sex and marriage by then.

"Damn Carter for being so stubborn!" she said out loud, hoping anger might help her find a little energy. But the mention of his name only brought fresh tears to her eyes, and a craving for more ice cream. "Pathetic," she mumbled as she shuffled toward the kitchen. "I'm just pathetic."

The insistent ring of the doorbell shattered the midday silence, pulling Joni from her stupor. Shoving the ice cream carton back into the freezer, she stared at the front door. If she ignored the summons, maybe whoever was on the other side would go away.

What if it was Carter? Her heart raced at the thought. She didn't want to talk to him, but if she could just see him, maybe she'd feel better. At least then she'd know he was all right.

The bell sounded again. She tiptoed to the door and stretched up to peer through the peephole. Instead of Carter's handsome face, G.P. stood on the landing, hands on her hips. "Joni, I know you're in there," she said. "You'd better open this door before I call the building manager to let me in."

Busted. No way would she get away with ignoring

G.P. She slid back the chain and turned the lock. "Hello, G.P." she said as she held open the door.

G.P. took in Joni's ice-cream stained robe and pajama-clad legs. "Something tells me this is more than just a bad-hair day," she said. She marched past Joni and deposited her purse on the coffee table, then took a seat on the sofa and patted the cushion beside her. "Come tell me what's wrong."

Joni swallowed the lump in her throat. "D-on't you think a man shouldn't love his job more than he loves you?"

G.P.'s eyes narrowed. "I should have known this was man trouble the minute I saw the chocolate ice-cream stains." She patted the cushion beside her more forcefully. "Now sit down and tell me everything that happened."

Joni shuffled over and sat, aware of G.P.'s keen eyes studying her. "We had a fight," she said.

"Give me credit, child. I figured out that much. A fight about his job, I take it."

Joni nodded. "You were right when you said I'd fallen in love with him. And he said he loved me." She swallowed another knot of tears. "I finally worked up the nerve to admit that and everything was going so well. The only thing that could possibly keep us from being happy was his job. I thought if he left the police force and did something else..."

Her voice failed her in the face of G.P.'s horrified look. "And you thought he'd go along with the idea? One look and I'd have told you he had more spine than that." She shook her head. "A man who does something just because you say so isn't a man you want to have."

"It wasn't like that," she protested. "I thought he'd agree with the idea because he wanted it, too." She clenched her hands in her lap, digging her fingernails into her palms. "G.P., if you could have seen him the other night when he came over here. He'd had a horrible evening. A boy he'd been trying to help died. I couldn't stand to see how much he was hurting." She glanced at her grandmother. "If he wasn't a police officer, he'd never have to go through that again."

G.P. laid her hand on Joni's clenched fists. "You don't know that, dear. Life is full of all kinds of pain. That's part of living."

She hung her head. "Carter said something like that, too. But why go out of your way to court pain?"

She could feel G.P.'s gaze on her, but her grandmother remained silent. When she finally spoke, her voice was gentle. "Do you remember when you were a little girl, about eight years old, I think, and your parents gave you a parakeet for your birthday? You were crazy about that little bird. You taught it to say all sorts of things and to sit on your shoulder while you walked around the house."

Joni stared at G.P. "His name was Perry. I haven't thought about him in a long time."

G.P. nodded. "You had Perry about three years when he died. You were inconsolable. You cried so much your mother worried you'd make yourself sick.

I offered to buy you another bird, but you wouldn't hear of it. You said you never wanted another one because it hurt too much when they were gone." G.P. patted her hand. "You always took things so to heart, child."

"You say that as if it's a bad thing."

"It's only bad if it keeps you from enjoying life the way you should. From letting yourself love, even when it hurts."

Joni looked away. "I don't know if I can do that."

G.P. sighed. "I'm old and I'm supposed to be full of all this wisdom for you young people, but I don't know if I can even make you understand. But I'll try."

She stared into the distance, as if looking back in time. "You already know that when I met your grandfather he was a daredevil pilot. He flew rickety old planes all over the country, performing at air shows and anywhere people would pay to see him. It was crazy, foolhardy work, and he loved every minute of it. His ability to seize hold of life and squeeze every bit of enjoyment he could from it was one of the things I loved most about him. If I had tried to take that from him by clipping his wings, he would have been a different man than the one I fell in love with."

"I know what you're saying, but I'm not like you. I can't just stand by waiting for something awful to happen."

"Listen, child. I haven't finished." G.P. squeezed Joni's arm. "Even when he wasn't flying in air shows, George was happiest in a plane. He flew reconnaissance for the border patrol or dusted crops or anything that would take him up in a plane."

"And he ended up dying that way," Joni said. "I remember how devastated you were."

"Yes, I was." The lines around her mouth deepened. "I wished I'd died right along with him. But that didn't make me regret one minute we'd spent together."

She pulled Joni's hands into her lap and looked into her eyes. "Knowing that what George did was dangerous—that any day he climbed into that plane he could be taken from me—made us value our time together all the more. We never took each other for granted, and every moment was sweet." She squeezed Joni's hands and smiled. "You can have that with Carter, too. But you have to be willing to take the chance."

Joni looked away. "I...I don't know if I can." How could you keep moving forward in a relationship, knowing the future held so much danger?

"You can do it. You're stronger than you think. And if you're willing to risk your heart that way, the love that comes back to you will be that much richer and more precious."

Joni put her arms around her grandmother and held her close. "I wish I had your faith," she said. "But I don't think I do."

"I have something that might help." She gently pushed Joni away and reached around to fish something from the neck of her blouse. "Your grandfather gave me this necklace as a wedding present, and I've worn it every day since." She slipped a simple knotted cord from around her neck and draped it over Joni's head.

Joni fingered the rows of knots, unable to hide her puzzlement.

"It's made out of the ripcord of a parachute," G.P. said. "He said when he gave it to me it was a reminder that he had a very good reason for staying alive up there in that plane—that I was like his parachute, keeping him safe. Whenever I looked at it, I thought of the commitment we'd made to each other."

She smiled and Joni had a sudden vision of the beautiful young woman her grandmother had been, a young woman willing to risk everything to be with the man she loved. "We were so lucky. How many people find that kind of love in their lives? It doesn't matter if it's for a day or a year. You can only live in the present."

Joni looked down at the necklace again. "Part of me wants to believe you're right. But the rest of me needs more time to get used to the idea."

G.P. patted her shoulder. "Then take your time. But don't take too long. Even good men like Carter get impatient."

She stood and looked down at Joni. "Now get dressed and I'll take you out for a decent meal."

"You don't have to do that."

"Yes, I do. I don't intend to let you continue to sit

around moping and eating junk food, any more than I intended to allow you to let you waste time dating boring men who are totally unsuitable for you." She grinned at Joni's surprised look. "You may balk at my meddling, but you have to admit my visit here led you to meeting the right man after all, and that's all I ask for."

"Nothing's settled yet, G.P." Her grandmother could talk all she wanted to about courage, but right now Joni still felt like a coward. A coward who needed to guard her heart from any more pain.

"Then I'll have to stay in town a little longer, won't I?" G.P. made a shooing motion. "We'll eat steak and talk about the wedding."

Joni rolled her eyes and heaved herself off the couch. There was no sense arguing with G.P. She could plan weddings to her heart's content, but that didn't mean one would take place. Joni's future happiness, or lack of it, was in Carter's hands now.

12

JONI SPENT the next twenty-four hours thinking about G.P.'s advice and trying to decide what to do. She cleaned the apartment and washed dishes and clothes, wishing it was as easy to clean up the mess she'd made of her love life. G.P. made it sound so simple, as if all she had to do was make up her mind to look at life and love from a different perspective and everything would be perfect. But what was easy about that? Part of her really wanted to be more accepting of Carter's job, but her old fears managed to keep a firm hold on her heart.

When the doorbell rang that afternoon, she was sure it was G.P. checking up on her. But when she opened the door, Carter was standing there, looking both handsome and forbidding in his uniform, no sign of a smile in sight.

"Uh, hello." She searched his eyes for some sign of his intentions, but he remained impassive.

"I'm here because you still owe me a date," he said.

"I do?" She stepped back, opening the door wider. "You aren't exactly dressed for a date."

"I'm dressed for the kind of date I have in mind."

She raised one eyebrow. "Are you going to arrest me?"

The heated look he gave her sent a flutter through her stomach. "I can think of a few things I'd like to do with you and a pair of handcuffs, but taking you to jail isn't one of them."

She lifted her chin, trying to pretend his words hadn't melted her from the inside out. "Then what did you have in mind?"

"Come with me and I'll show you." He held out his hand.

She took another step back. "Can I trust you?"

He dropped his hand. "You tell me."

So maybe she deserved that. She looked away. She trusted Carter, but could she trust herself to be alone with him and think clearly? "Where are we going?"

"You'll see. Get your purse and come with me." He hesitated, then added, "Please."

His plea won her over. She retrieved her purse and followed him out the door to his truck. Neither said anything on the drive to the police station. She told herself she was ready for anything he might throw at her. When he pulled into the employee parking lot, she turned to him. "What now?"

"You're going on a ride-along."

"You mean I'm going to work with you?" That was one possibility she hadn't thought of.

"That's right." His eyes met hers. "Before you make up your mind completely about my job—about us—I want you to see what I really do."

Her stomach gave a nervous flutter. Was she ready for this? She nodded. "All right. That's fair enough."

She followed him into the station, back to a desk where he handed her a sheaf of papers. "What's this?" she asked.

"Essentially, they want enough information to run you through the computers and make sure you're not some felon, and then you have to agree not to blame the PD for anything that happens while you're out there with me."

She accepted the papers. "And what might happen?"

He studied her through half-closed eyes, his voice a seductive growl. "When you're with me—anything."

She laughed and filled out the paperwork, then followed him into a large meeting room where a dozen or more officers clutching clipboards and coffee mugs milled about. "Briefing is where we get our assignments and catch up on what's going on in the department and on the streets," he explained. "Not particularly exciting for us, but I've noticed civilians seem to get a kick out of it."

"I'm sure I'll find it fascinating."

She took a seat at the back while he went forward with half-a-dozen other officers. There was some good-natured ribbing about her presence there, then the conversation turned more serious, with several officers offering their condolences on the death of Tino.

It was obvious Carter was liked and respected.

Why, then, did she think of him as a loner? Maybe it was because she had some prejudiced image of him as a tough-guy cop who never let anyone close to him.

But she should have known better. Because with her, he held nothing back. It made her realize what a special gift he'd given to her.

He looked back over his shoulder and smiled at her. That brief curve of his lips made her feel lighter than air, and she wondered if the look on her face was as goofy as it felt.

The patrol sergeant who conducted the briefing was brisk and thorough, rattling off assignments, call signs and car numbers for the day at a dizzying rate. He gave information on suspects in various open cases and announced an upcoming training class. Half an hour and pages of notes later, they were dismissed.

The noise level in the room rose immediately, as officers switched on radios and gathered up supplies. Joni was reminded of the emergency room whenever a critical case came in; everyone had a job to do and was in a hurry to do it.

"You ready to roll?" Carter approached her, what looked like a salesman's sample case in his hand.

"Whenever you are. What's in the case?"

"Supplies. Paperwork, evidence bags, tickets, gloves, crime-scene tape. Whatever we might need at a crime scene." He winked. "And I'll bet you thought all I needed was my gun and my personal charm."

"They worked for me." She followed him outside to a familiar SAPD patrol car. How many times had she seen these white cars with black-and-yellow markings on the street and thought only that she was grateful this one hadn't flagged her down to write her a speeding ticket? After tonight, she had a feeling she wouldn't think of them the same way again.

He opened the back seat and deposited the case inside. She was surprised to see that the seat was one piece of molded plastic, like a waiting room bench. "Easier to clean," Carter said, seeing her surprise. "And no place to stash contraband." He led her around to the back of the car. "You'd better put your purse in the trunk."

She didn't know what she'd expected to find in the trunk, but it wasn't the row of plastic-wrapped teddy bears that greeted her. She grinned. "Stuffed animals?"

"We give them to children at crime scenes. It gives them something to hold on to and helps calm them down." He pointed to a stack of what looked like blankets in the corner. "We have afghans for the adults, too." She recalled seeing patients come into the E.R. wrapped in afghans, but she'd never connected them to the police.

He shut the trunk and they got into the car. Carter immediately began flipping switches and adjusting the sound level of various radios. Rock music blared from one speaker. "This station all right?"

"You have a radio? I mean, a real radio?"

"You listen to the radio at your office, don't you?"

"Yes, when we're not too busy."

"Same here. This is my office. In fact, you're sitting on my desk." The suggestive look he gave her made her laugh.

He keyed the radio mike. "Two-Adam-One, in service."

"Two-Adam-One, copy, at fifteen thirty-one."

"What do you do now?" she asked as he turned the car onto the street.

"Basically, I drive around looking for anything suspicious. I can make traffic stops, follow up on previous cases, do bar checks...it's pretty much up to me, as long as I'm available to handle radio calls and to back up other officers on calls."

"I can see how this job would appeal to someone who likes his independence." But then, a lot of other jobs offered independence, and no one ever shot at you, she thought.

She settled back in the seat and listened to the constant chatter of the police radio. From this perspective, the whole city was a hotbed of criminal activity, from speeding drivers to shoplifters to shootings. And to think most of this stuff never even made the paper.

After half an hour of driving around, Carter steered the car into a lot and parked. "Time to take a walk," he said. He keyed the mike. "Show me code six at Quintano Park on a citizen contact for a few. Code four."

Joni watched people's reactions as they walked down the street. Some of them smiled or nodded in greeting. Others ignored them and looked the other way. More than a few crossed the street to avoid them. And at least two women looked Carter up and down with open appreciation. Joni moved closer to him. "Do you get hit on a lot?" she asked.

"Some." He grinned at her. "Does it bother you?"

"Why should it bother me?" She glared at a long-legged beanpole who looked a little too interested.

He laughed. "You don't have anything to worry about. Badge bunnies don't interest me."

At the end of the street, he turned in to a small park where a group of kids sat or lay in the shade of a scraggly oak. The kids watched their approach warily, their faces relaxing as they drew nearer. "Hey, Carter," one said.

"How's it going, Andy? Petra. Joey." One by one, he greeted each kid by name. Joni wondered how many adults saw these outcasts, with their dirty clothes and matted hair, their sullen looks and defensive posturing, and thought of them as children with names and feelings, and stories of their own.

She was aware of their eyes on her, questioning. "Who's the babe?" a boy named Talon asked.

"This is a friend of mine, Joni. She's riding with me today."

"What kind of friend?" A girl with a bandage on her hand, Angel, asked.

Carter smiled at her. "A very good one."

A couple of kids laughed then and made remarks that had her blushing. Carter quickly turned the conversation more serious. "Any VKs been around making trouble?" he asked.

"Not any more than usual." Joey, a tall boy with dreadlocks, stood and shoved his hands into his pockets. "The only people who really hassle us are the business owners around here."

Carter nodded. "We've had complaints about kids loitering in front of their doors, hassling their customers for change."

"We aren't hurtin' anybody." Petra glared at him, defiant.

"Maybe not. But you'll make it easier on everybody if you move around some. You can always go over to the Rec Center or to The Spot."

"The Spot's only open at night these days," Andy said. "They got their funding cut."

"If Mr. Store Owner don't like us hangin' out, he ought to send some of his money over there so they can keep the doors open more," Petra said.

"I may have said something along those lines when I talked to him," Carter said. He looked around the group. "Anybody seen Luz lately?"

"I saw her yesterday," Angel said. "She was spanging over on Culebra and General McMullen." She hung her head. "I heard what happened to Tino. That sucks."

"Word is you were with him when he bought it," Joey said.

Carter nodded. "I was. But I got there too late."

"Ain't your fault. The dude didn't trust nobody."

"You get burned enough times, you learn not to trust," Carter said.

Petra looked sad. "At least you tried to help."

"We'd better be moving along now," Carter said. He started to turn away, then stopped and looked at Angel. "The clinic on Naco Perrin can give you something for that hand. They won't charge if you tell them I sent you. Do you need a ride over there?"

She shook her head. "No, I can get there on my own."

When they were back on the main street, Joni turned to him. "What's The Spot? And what's 'spanging'?"

"Spanging is begging for spare change. It's the main way the kids get money, unless they turn tricks or steal stuff and sell it. Some of them do all three. The Spot is a youth shelter set up by the city. There's a basketball court, a soup kitchen, a dormitory and study hall. Kids can study for their GED, get a meal or a change of clothes, condoms or needle kits."

"Sounds like a pretty ambitious program."

"It is. But there's never enough money or human resources for everything that's needed."

They walked on in silence. Though Carter's eyes constantly assessed their surroundings, she wondered how much of his thoughts were with the children they'd just left. "It must be frustrating for you, not to be able to help them more," she said.

He nodded. "But it has its moments."

"How many of them get off the street?"

"Last year? Six."

"Out of how many?"

"Maybe sixty. There're more I never come in contact with."

"Ten percent is a pretty low rate of return."

He glanced at her, challenge in his eyes. "That's six kids who didn't die or end up in jail."

They returned to the car and headed back out. As Carter drove down side streets and slowed to look into alleys, Joni realized he was searching for something. Or someone. "What are you looking for?" she asked.

He slowed to check the loading dock behind a shuttered warehouse. "Luz. I haven't seen her since the shooting. I want to make sure she's all right."

The worry in his voice told her more than his words how much this meant to him. "When you look at them, you see yourself, don't you? The kid *you* were."

He glanced at her and nodded. "I never thought about it that way, but I guess you're right. I *know* what they're feeling. What they're going through. There aren't many people who can say that. That's why it's important for me to be there for them."

Could you be there for them in the same way if you weren't a cop? she wanted to ask, but she didn't. She thought she already knew the answer. Her earlier assumption that he was in this job for thrills seemed petty now. Compassion and empathy, not a love of violence or risk, drove him to do this. And hadn't she recognized those qualities in him from the very first?

G.P.'s words came back to her: *If I had tried to take that from him by clipping his wings, he would have been a different man than the one I fell in love with.*

"There she is."

Joni had to search the crowded sidewalk for several seconds before she spotted the short, thin girl sitting with her back against the brick wall of a store, her hand extended, palm up, in a silent plea.

Carter pulled the car to the curb and rolled down the window. "*Hola*, Luz."

Luz watched as they got out of the car and came over to her. "Luz, I'd like you to meet a friend of mine, Joni. Joni, this is Luz."

She was a slight, pretty girl, with long black hair and delicate features. Her face was flushed, her eyes red as if she'd been crying. Carter squatted in front of her. "How are you doing?"

She shrugged. "I'm okay."

"You don't look okay."

"Yeah, well, I think I'm getting a cold."

He glanced around them. "You having any luck today?"

"Some." Her eyes darted away from him, then back. "I heard Tino's funeral is tomorrow."

He nodded. "You need a ride to the service?"

She looked down. "Yeah. That'd be good."

"None of the VKs have been hassling you, have they?"

She shook her head.

"If they do, or if you need anything else, you can call me. Anytime. You have my card?"

"I still got it."

He rocked back on his heels. "School starts next week. The youth shelter has a bed open if you want to go."

She hugged her arms across her body. "I been thinking about it. I don't know, though..."

"If you're tough enough to make it out here, you're tough enough to get through high school.

"Maybe."

Carter straightened. "I'll pick you up tomorrow about one and we'll go to the funeral. We'll talk more then. Maybe I'll run you by the shelter, so you can see it."

She nodded. "Okay."

He pulled a five from his pocket and pressed it into her hand. "Go get something to eat. I'll see you tomorrow."

After five minutes, Joni couldn't stand Carter's silence any longer. "Do you think Luz will get off the streets and go back to school?"

"I think she will. She's a smart kid."

You deserve most of the credit if she does, she thought. But she didn't say it. He wasn't the type who wanted praise for what he did. She fingered her grandmother's necklace, wondering if G.P. had felt this kind of pride and overwhelming tenderness for her high-flying husband.

"I don't remember seeing that necklace before. What is it, some kind of macramé or something?"

She pulled the necklace out where he could see it. "It's a parachute cord. G.P. gave it to me. My grandfather gave it to her when they were married."

He glanced at her again. "Why did she give it to you?"

"I think for her it was a symbol of the love she and my grandfather had for each other—no matter what else happened to them." She studied the knotted cord, a feeling in her chest as if she was about to jump out into space, with no guarantee of a net beneath her. She cleared her throat. "She thought it would remind me of what's important in a relationship."

He reached over and turned down the radio. "And what is that?"

"I think...I think it's remembering that all the external stuff—jobs and family and other people—only affect you as much as you let them." She traced her finger around one of the knots. She could feel the corresponding tangle of her emotions unsnarling, the wisdom of her grandmother's words finally clear to her. "If you keep the focus on your love for each other, and make the most of every moment together, then the other stuff doesn't matter so much."

He reached for the radio mike. "Headquarters, Two-Adam-One."

"Two-Adam-One, go ahead."

"You have any calls holding?"

"That's negative, sir."

"Two-Adam-One copies. Hold me out for fifteen or so."

"Headquarters copies. Seventeen-oh-eight."

He turned into a lot behind an office building and backed into a space against the wall. "Why are we stopping?" Joni asked.

"Because I didn't think it would look so good if I stopped in the middle of the street to kiss you." He unfastened his seat belt and leaned toward her. When their lips met, she felt weak with relief. She'd come so close to losing him, all because of her foolish fears.

She slipped her arms around his neck and pulled him closer. It was like hugging a tree trunk, hard and unyielding. She smiled. "You're wearing your vest, aren't you?"

"I told you I always do."

Her smile broadened, and the lightness in her chest expanded. "I love you," she whispered.

He drew back enough to look into her eyes. "Enough to be a cop's wife?"

She caught her breath, surprise and joy threatening to overwhelm her. "I...it still scares me, but yes, I do."

He kissed her again and she felt as if his arms around her were the only reasons she wasn't floating right out of the car. He stroked one finger across a knot in the necklace. "I think I'd better send G.P. the biggest bunch of roses I can find," he said.

"Pink is her favorite color." She kissed him again,

teasing him with her tongue. "Mmm. I've never made out in a cop car before."

"See, there are all kinds of benefits to hanging out with the good guys."

"Such as?"

"We have real handcuffs."

She laughed and kissed him again. She hugged him close, and tried to freeze the moment in her mind. This was what she wanted to remember in the future, when the old fears crept in to paralyze her. This was what she wanted to cherish, this love that was more powerful than fear, more thrilling than any kind of danger.

Epilogue

Three months later

"COME ON, CARTER, wake up! We'll be late!" Joni gave his shoulder a shake.

Carter covered Joni's hand with his own and tried to roll back over in bed. "Be late for what?" He pulled her back down beside him and slid his free hand across the curve of her breast. "Why don't we just stay in bed?"

She laughed and pulled away. "Save some for the honeymoon."

His smile sent a rush of heat through her. "Oh, there's plenty more where that came from."

She swatted his shoulder. "You have to get up now. We have to be at the airport at nine."

With a groan, he shoved himself into a sitting position and scratched his chin. "I can't believe you're really going through with this."

She sat on the side of the bed and began pulling on socks. "The wedding or this morning?"

"Both." He crawled out of bed and stretched his arms over his head. "Tell me again why we're doing this?"

The sight of his lean, muscular body stretched out

in front of her rendered her momentarily speechless. How was it that the longer she knew him, the more she lusted after this man?

"Is there a hidden daredevil in you I know nothing about?" He nudged her shoulder.

She glanced up at him. "I don't think so, though G.P. says I might surprise myself one day."

"Oh, so this was G.P.'s idea. I might have known."

"No, it's my idea." She stood and began pulling on a pair of jeans.

"Which brings me back to my original question." He reached for his own clothes. "Why this sudden urge to jump out of a plane two days before our wedding?"

She fingered the parachute cord necklace. "Consider it practice for the real thing."

"How's that?" He frowned, obviously puzzled.

"Today we're jumping out of a plane together. Two days from now, we're taking an even bigger leap of faith."

"I think G.P.'s right. There is a hidden daredevil in you." He tried to pull her close once more.

She shoved away. "I know what you're doing. You're stalling." She stared at him, understanding dawning. "Carter Sullivan—you're scared!"

"Me?" He took a step back. "Why would you think that?"

She grabbed his hands. "Your fingers are freezing." She raised her eyes to meet his. "You really are scared, aren't you?"

He nodded. "Terrified."

She smiled. "Then you know how I feel about the wedding."

He returned the smile. "Guess there's only one thing to do, then."

"What's that?"

He pulled her close and wrapped his arms around her. "Get through this together." He brushed his fingers across her mouth. "Is screaming allowed?"

She grinned. "Only in bed."

He slid one hand down her back to cup her bottom. "I thought I was supposed to make you scream."

"It works both ways."

He nuzzled her neck. "I think I'm going to like this."

"Skydiving or marriage?"

"With you—both."

Is your man too good to be true?

Hot, gorgeous AND romantic?
If so, he could be a Harlequin® Blaze™ series cover model!

Our grand-prize winners will receive a trip for two to New York City to
shoot the cover of a Blaze novel, and will stay at the luxurious Plaza Hotel.
Plus, they'll receive $500 U.S. spending money!
The runner-up winners will receive $200 U.S.
to spend on a romantic dinner for two.

It's easy to enter!

In 100 words or less, tell us what makes your boyfriend or spouse a true romantic
and the perfect candidate for the cover of a Blaze novel, and include in your submission
two photos of this potential cover model.

All entries must include the written submission of the contest entrant, two photographs of the model
candidate and the Official Entry Form and Publicity Release forms completed in full and signed by
both the model candidate and the contest entrant. Harlequin, along with the experts at
Elite Model Management, will select a winner.

For photo and complete Contest details, please refer to the Official Rules on the next page. All entries
will become the property of Harlequin Enterprises Ltd. and are not returnable.

**Please visit www.blazecovermodel.com to download a copy of the Official Entry Form and
Publicity Release Form or send a request to one of the addresses below.**

Please mail your entry to: **Harlequin Blaze Cover Model Search**

In U.S.A.	In Canada
P.O. Box 9069	P.O. Box 637
Buffalo, NY	Fort Erie, ON
14269-9069	L2A 5X3

No purchase necessary. Contest open to Canadian and U.S. residents who are 18 and over.
Void where prohibited. Contest closes September 30, 2003.

HARLEQUIN BLAZE COVER MODEL SEARCH CONTEST 3569 OFFICIAL RULES
NO PURCHASE NECESSARY TO ENTER

1. To enter, submit two (2) 4" x 6" photographs of a boyfriend or spouse (who must be 18 years of age or older) taken no later than three (3) months from the time of entry: a close-up, waist up, shirtless photograph; and a fully clothed, full-length photograph, then, tell us, in 100 words or fewer, why he should be a Harlequin Blaze cover model and how he is romantic. Your complete "entry" must include: (i) your essay, (ii) the Official Entry Form and Publicity Release Form printed below completed and signed by you (as "Entrant"), (iii) the photographs (with your hand-written name, address and phone number, and your model's name, address and phone number on the back of each photograph), and (iv) the Publicity Release Form and Photograph Representation Form printed below completed and signed by your model (as "Model"), and should be sent via first-class mail to either: Harlequin Blaze Cover Model Search Contest 3569, P.O. Box 9069, Buffalo, NY, 14269-9069, or Harlequin Blaze Cover Model Search Contest 3569, P.O. Box 637, Fort Erie, Ontario L2A 5X3. All submissions must be in English and be received no later than September 30, 2003. Limit: one entry per person, household or organization. **Purchase or acceptance of a product offer does not improve your chances of winning.** All entry requirements must be strictly adhered to for eligibility and to ensure fairness among entries.

2. Ten (10) Finalist submissions (photographs and essays) will be selected by a panel of judges consisting of members of the Harlequin editorial, marketing and public relations staff, as well as a representative from Elite Model Management (Toronto) Inc., based on the following criteria:

Aptness/Appropriateness of submitted photographs for a Harlequin Blaze cover—70%

Originality of Essay—20%

Sincerity of Essay—10%

In the event of a tie, duplicate finalists will be selected. The photographs submitted by finalists will be posted on the Harlequin website no later than November 15, 2003 (at www.blazecovermodel.com), and viewers may vote, in rank order, on their favorite(s) to assist in the panel of judges' final determination of the Grand Prize and Runner-up winning entries based on the above judging criteria. All decisions of the judges are final.

3. All entries become the property of Harlequin Enterprises Ltd. and none will be returned. Any entry may be used for future promotional purposes. Elite Model Management (Toronto) Inc. and/or its partners, subsidiaries and affiliates operating as "Elite Model Management" will have access to all entries including all personal information, and may contact any Entrant and/or Model in its sole discretion for their own business purposes. Harlequin and Elite Model Management (Toronto) Inc. are separate entities with no legal association or partnership whatsoever having no power to bind or obligate the other or create any expressed or implied obligation or responsibility on behalf of the other, such that Harlequin shall not be responsible in any way for any acts or omissions of Elite Model Management (Toronto) Inc. or its partners, subsidiaries and affiliates in connection with the Contest or otherwise and Elite Model Management shall not be responsible in any way for any acts or omissions of Harlequin or its partners, subsidiaries and affiliates in connection with the contest or otherwise.

4. All Entrants and Models must be residents of the U.S. or Canada, be 18 years of age or older, and have no prior criminal convictions. The contest is not open to any Model that is a professional model and/or actor in any capacity at the time of the entry. Contest void wherever prohibited by law; all applicable laws and regulations apply. Any litigation within the Province of Quebec regarding the conduct or organization of a publicity contest may be submitted to the Régie des alcools, des courses et des jeux for a ruling, and any litigation regarding the awarding of a prize may be submitted to the Régie only for the purpose of helping the parties reach a settlement. Employees and immediate family members of Harlequin Enterprises Ltd., D.L. Blair, Inc., Elite Model Management (Toronto) Inc. and their parents, affiliates, subsidiaries and all other agencies, entities and persons connected with the use, marketing or conduct of this Contest are not eligible to enter. Acceptance of any prize offered constitutes permission to use Entrants' and Models' names, essay submissions, photographs or other likenesses for the purposes of advertising, trade, publication and promotion on behalf of Harlequin Enterprises Ltd., its parent, affiliates, subsidiaries, assigns and other authorized entities involved in the judging and promotion of the contest without further compensation to any Entrant or Model, unless prohibited by law.

5. Finalists will be determined no later than October 30, 2003. Prize Winners will be determined no later than January 31, 2004. Grand Prize Winners (consisting of winning Entrant and Model) will be required to sign and return Affidavit of Eligibility/Release of Liability and Model Release forms within thirty (30) days of notification. Non-compliance with this requirement and within the specified time period will result in disqualification and an alternate will be selected. Any prize notification returned as undeliverable will result in the awarding of the prize to an alternate set of winners. All travelers (or parent/legal guardian of a minor) must execute the Affidavit of Eligibility/Release of Liability prior to ticketing and must possess required travel documents (e.g. valid photo ID) where applicable. Travel dates specified by Sponsor but no later than May 30, 2004.

6. Prizes: One (1) Grand Prize—the opportunity for the Model to appear on the cover of a paperback book from the Harlequin Blaze series, and a 3 day/2 night trip for two (Entrant and Model) to New York, NY for the photo shoot of Model which includes round-trip coach air transportation from the commercial airport nearest the winning Entrant's home to New York, NY, (or, in lieu of air transportation, $100 cash payable to Entrant and Model, if the winning Entrant's home is within 250 miles of New York, NY), hotel accommodations (double occupancy) at the Plaza Hotel and $500 cash spending money payable to Entrant and Model, (approximate prize value: $8,000), and one (1) Runner-up Prize of $200 cash payable to Entrant and Model for a romantic dinner for two (approximate prize value: $200). Prizes are valued in U.S. currency. Prizes consist of only those items listed as part of the prize. No substitution of prize(s) permitted by winners. All prizes are awarded jointly to the Entrant and Model of the winning entries, and are not severable - prizes and obligations may not be assigned or transferred. Any change to the Entrant and/or Model of the winning entries will result in disqualification and an alternate will be selected. Taxes on prize are the sole responsibility of winners. Any and all expenses and/or items not specifically described as part of the prize are the sole responsibility of winners. Harlequin Enterprises Ltd. and D.L. Blair, Inc., their parents, affiliates, and subsidiaries are not responsible for errors in printing of Contest entries and/or game pieces. No responsibility is assumed for lost, stolen, late, illegible, incomplete, inaccurate, non-delivered, postage due or misdirected mail or entries. In the event of printing or other errors which may result in unintended prize values or duplication of prizes, all affected game pieces or entries shall be null and void.

7. Winners will be notified by mail. For winners' list (available after March 31, 2004), send a self-addressed, stamped envelope to: Harlequin Blaze Cover Model Search Contest 3569 Winners, P.O. Box 4200, Blair, NE 68009-4200, or refer to the Harlequin website (at www.blazecovermodel.com).

Contest sponsored by Harlequin Enterprises Ltd., P.O. Box 9042, Buffalo, NY 14269-9042.

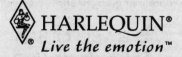

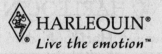

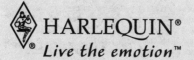

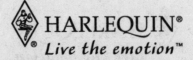